The Shades of Us Trilogy Book 1

Scarlet Whispers

ABBY FARNSWORTH

This is a work of fiction. Names, characters, places, and incidents are products of the author's imagination or are used fictitiously and are not to be construed as real. Any resemblance to actual events, locations, organizations, or persons, living or dead, is entirely coincidental.

World Castle Publishing, LLC
Pensacola, Florida
Copyright © Abby Farnsworth 2022
Hardback ISBN: 9798832530239
Paperback ISBN: 9781958336175
eBook ISBN: 9781958336182
First Edition World Castle Publishing, LLC, June 20, 2022
http://www.worldcastlepublishing.com
Licensing Notes
Cover: Karen Fuller
Editor: Maxine Bringenberg

Table of Contents

Prologue   6
Chapter 1 — A Million Years   13
Chapter 2 — Just a Dance   24
Chapter 3 — Pretend   39
Chapter 4 — Cruel Temptations   48
Chapter 5 — You're a...   59
Chapter 6 — Fortress   71
Chapter 7 — The Challenge   83
Chapter 8 — So Finite   99
Chapter 9 — Change Him   104
Chapter 10 — Precious Heartbeat   111
Chapter 11 — Split in Two   118
Chapter 12 — Now   125
Chapter 13 — Run   137
Chapter 14 — A Girl   143
Chapter 15 — Bloodlust   155
Chapter 16 — My Everything   162
Chapter 17 — Freezing   173
Chapter 18 — Marriage   178
Chapter 19 — In Love With You   184
Chapter 20 — Forever   196

Acknowledgments

Thank you to Karen Fuller, Maxine Bringenberg, and World Castle Publishing! I'm so thankful to be one of your authors! Thank you to my mom, dad, family, and readers. Your reviews, support, and encouragement mean so much! Another thank you to Jason McCrady and M.J. Lemon—your support is so appreciated! Also, thank you to Hermione Li and Missy Davis for encouraging me. Thank you to Ryan Smith for always supporting me. Finally, thank you again to my readers for writing reviews, purchasing my books, and staying with me!

To my EverGreen Trilogy readers, thank you for coming back! I'm so happy you decided to read my next trilogy. I hope you enjoy Anne, James, and Albert as much as you did my other characters. Happy reading!

To my new readers, thank you for choosing one of my books! I'm glad you decided to read Scarlet Whispers. I hope you enjoy your adventure with Anne, James, and Albert. If you do, go check out my first series, the EverGreen Trilogy. Enjoy!

Dedication

To my readers

"Because I could not stop for Death —
He kindly stopped for me —
The carriage held but just Ourselves —
And Immortality."

"Because I Could Not Stop For Death" by Emily
Dickinson

Prologue

The band was playing a slow, melancholy song. All the girls stood near the back wall, waiting to be asked to dance. As boys came up to them with nervous smiles, the girls giggled and happily accepted their offers. A slow dance was the one time a girl never wanted to be left alone. Under the soft glow of the lights, love could blossom. That was the dream of so many of the girls I knew. Many of them had high hopes for this dance.

Candles adorned the room, causing it to sparkle. The floor was shiny and bright, almost like a true ballroom. I felt like a European countess. Closing my eyes, I imagined I was in London. I had always wanted to visit the United Kingdom. The smell of roses enveloped my senses in a flurry of sweetness. It was surreal, almost magical.

A few of my friends were huddled off to the side, whispering about several of the popular boys from school. My cousin, Claudia, was particularly interested in a black-haired boy from literature class. He'd just asked her to dance, and she was practically glowing. I smiled at them as they walked onto the dance floor. Claudia looked back at me and grinned as he gently placed his hand on her waist. Who knew? Maybe they'd fall in love.

I didn't have to worry about being a wallflower. Glen would be there any second. I looked down at my scarlet dress and baby-doll heels. A black velvet ribbon, the same color as my pinned-up curls, was tied around my waist. Briefly glancing at a mirror on the wall beside me, I examined my lipstick. Thankfully, it was still the same strawberry-red color it had been when I had first put it on. I wanted to be beautiful.

Just as I reached up to adjust my hair, he was behind me. His familiar cologne flooded my senses with hints of cinnamon and cherry. Glen's hand found its way into mine as I turned around to face him. Sweet, familiar brown eyes gazed into mine as he smiled at me. As I leaned closer to him, I imagined his heart beating next to mine.

"Anne, you're gorgeous," he whispered.

That was exactly what I wanted to hear. I loved him so much. If he thought I was beautiful, I'd be content. I so badly wanted to marry this gorgeous, ever-loving man.

Glen's voice was soft and gentle, and his breath smelled of coffee and sugar. When he smiled, I imagined that I was glimpsing an angel. My heart was his.

I glanced down at the floor. "Thank you."

"Are you ready to dance?" he asked.

His familiar smile was bright and steady. As always, he made me forget everyone else in the room. It was as if it really was just the two of us.

He was the prince, and I was the princess. I pretended we were in our own castle, twirling around the floor. Maybe I could be Cinderella or even Sleeping Beauty. It didn't matter, though, as long as Glen was my prince.

I smiled at him. "Oh, yes."

The dance floor was full of young couples. It had been five years since the war, but people still hadn't forgotten what it was like to not have dances, carnivals, and parties. I had only been twelve when the war ended, but even I remembered the disturbing absence of young men. My cousins had been shipped overseas to fight the Germans, and just like that, there were no men in my family between the ages of eighteen and thirty-five left at home.

I had known Glen back then, too. He, along with all the other boys, had been so angry to be left at home. At the time, I had looked at him like he was crazy. I had always wondered why anyone would ever want to be sent to fight in such a dangerous, deadly war. And even then, I hadn't wanted to lose him. But now, I found his new uniform incredibly handsome.

His defense of our country was so attractive, his strong arms demanded attention. Oh, he was wonderful. Did he even know how much I loved him? Most likely not, because I couldn't even manage to utter the words 'I love you.'

I was only a few days shy of my eighteenth birthday. Though I hadn't told anyone, I was hoping Glen would propose. We hadn't talked about it, but his mother adored me. He had talked to my father at length last night after dinner. I could only hope I was right.

I so badly wanted to don a tea-length gown, a white ribbon around my waist, and a pretty lace veil. I'd wear tall white heels and a pearl necklace around my throat. In my hands would be a bundle of white dahlias.

"You really do look nice tonight," he said.

I blushed. "You only think that because you're in love."

He laughed. "Well, you're right about one thing."

I grinned as he pulled me closer under the dim lights. My head fell softly against his shoulder. His arms wrapped around me as I let myself fall into him. I felt as if my heart might beat right out of my chest and into his hands. I had never been so in love. In fact, there had never been anyone else at all. Glen was my first and only boyfriend.

My life would be entirely wonderful if I could simply spend the rest of it with him. We'd have a few little children. Maybe a girl with his chocolate eyes and a boy with my raven hair. I'd walk around with a huge smile on my face as I felt our babies kick against my stomach. That would feel like heaven.

Perhaps we'd have a small country house. Maybe a few kittens or even a pony. I'd plant a flower garden, tending my rose bushes as they bloomed in the summer. The smell of apple pie would drift out our windows as I prepared our Sunday dinners. It would be picture-perfect. Almost like a fairytale.

And one day, we might have grandchildren. Our gray hair would remind us of our never-ending love. We'd laugh together as we reminisced about our peaceful life and the love we'd shared. It could be the picture of contentment.

A moment later, his hand tilted my chin up towards his. And then, our lips touched for the first time. I had never kissed anyone before. At first, I didn't know what to do. And if it had been anyone other than Glen, I probably would have been incredibly anxious. But when his soft lips met mine, all I felt was sheer happiness.

I had dreamed of this moment for so long. Part of me had doubted that it would ever happen. As he pulled away, I looked up into his eyes. He grinned down at me while his thumb stroked my cheek. My breath was coming out in short, heavy gasps.

"Anne," he whispered, "I love you so, so much."

Oh, yes! That was what I wanted. This was it! My dreams were coming true. What if he asked me? Would I be able to contain my excitement? Maybe not. I might collapse into a heap of giggles. Would he mind? Probably not. He would smile with me, wrapping me in his arms.

And he'd kiss me again!

The Second World War had brought so much sadness into my young life. Glen and I had both grown up in a world ravaged by war. We'd aged so quickly, losing our childhood innocence. But now, we finally had a chance at peace. And peace would be so much happier if we were together.

Our eyes were locked together as we admired each other's souls. His deep, chocolate eyes were dotted with caramel-colored specks. I imagined how my own sky-blue eyes must have looked to him.

I smiled brightly at him. "I love you, too."

Glen's hand was laced through mine as we stepped into the frigid air. My coat was pulled tightly around me, and I slipped my gloves on. It was exceptionally chilly. Glen had told my parents that he would bring me home. I had been particularly ecstatic about the arrangement. After all, a romantic car ride in the moonlight would be a lovely place to propose. All I could do was hope. There was a chance that within the next hour, my life would be changed forever.

Since the dance had been so crowded, Glen hadn't been able to park his car very close. As we turned down the little alley leading to where his car was parked, a shadowy figure, faster than anything I had ever seen before, darted in front of us. Glen saw it too and immediately threw himself in front of me. For a few seconds, we stood absolutely still. Then the figure appeared in front of us again. I screamed as Glen fell to the ground, blood dripping from the gash in his throat. The man I loved with all of my heart was bleeding to death in front of me. Panic coursed through my mind. I'm going to die, I thought. I wanted to run, hide, or scream for help, but I seemed to be frozen.

Only a fraction of a second later, I felt what seemed to be needles puncturing my throat. I was so incredibly dizzy. Everything appeared to spin as I was consumed by a floating sensation. My sense of time, space, and reality slowly faded away as I became filled with a total sense of relaxation. And just like that, I took my last mortal breath.

Chapter 1
A MILLION YEARS

He was here, again. Every single morning, he arrived in a polished suit. I'd seen him every day for years. And each time I brought him his vamp mimosa — lamb's blood with a dash of orange juice — he tried to flirt with me. If it had been anyone other than him, the most powerful vampire in Savannah, I probably would have slapped him by now. Not to say he wasn't attractive — he certainly was. Girls swooned over him when he walked by. Almost every girl wanted him, but that was the problem. He was a total player, and everyone knew it.

"Here you go," I said as I set his drink in front of him.

He looked up at me, his usual grin displayed on his face. His wavy brown hair fell gently across his forehead in a relaxed fashion. It was charming. There was no doubt about that. It would have been easy to give in to him.

"I don't suppose I could pay you enough to sit down with me and have one of these?" Albert asked.

I rolled my eyes. "Not in a million years."

He nodded as he took a sip. "That's what I thought."

I left him to his drink, walking back toward the kitchen. Katie, one of the cooks, glanced over at me. She shook her head, seemingly perplexed. Most people who knew of my odd relationship with Albert acted like that. No one quite understood why I always turned him down.

"Let me guess, he asked you again?" she said.

"Yep," I answered.

She sighed before responding. "Do you have any idea how many girls wish they were you? I mean, he's only the gorgeous, billionaire leader of the biggest coven in North America. Totally not a big deal."

Katie seemed slightly annoyed. Of course, that made sense since she'd been trying to convince me to go out with him from the first time he asked. Maybe she'd finally realized that her plan wasn't working out.

"He's arrogant and entitled," I replied.

"That certainly wouldn't bother me," Katie muttered in an exasperated tone.

I rolled my eyes and smiled before grabbing another food tray and walking out to the other seating area.

The Café De La Nuit had two seating areas. The main one, reserved for the human customers, was up front, close to the entrance. The second, a secluded room in the back of the building, was where we seated our other customers. Both rooms were gray, filled with small tables adorned with candles and succulents. The restaurant was a safe haven for many wolves and vamps in Savannah. It felt like a second home. That was one of the biggest reasons I enjoyed working there.

The restaurant owner was a well-to-do vampire who had been around for ages. Most of our staff were vamps, but we also had a few wolves, like Katie, on the payroll.

I delivered the stacks of pancakes to a young human family sitting near the front windows. One of the children, a little girl with bright blonde curls, smiled up at me.

"You're very pretty," she whispered.

I smiled at her. "Thank you."

I got that a lot. Humans weren't accustomed to seeing creatures with unblemished skin and clear, unearthly bright eyes. The compliments weren't so bad, but the catcalling by the endless number of creepy teenage boys was a bit annoying. Then again, it could have been worse.

At the end of the hour, I hung up my apron and dusted the crumbs off my skirt. I grabbed my purse out of the back room and headed toward the door. On my way out, I made eye contact with Albert. He gave me a slight nod as I walked toward the door. I lowered my eyes. By now, I had gotten used to it. After all, I'd learned that just about anything could happen in the twenty-first century.

Besides, Albert didn't really bother me. The only problem I had with him was his terrible reputation. And that wouldn't have been a problem, except that I knew the stories were true. So, so many girls had their hearts broken. It scared me, though I'd never tell him that.

Just as I opened the front door to step onto the sidewalk, someone ran into me and knocked me to the ground. My skirt flared around me as I landed on the hard, marble floor. I looked up to see a boy, maybe eighteen, standing over me. He looked intensely embarrassed. But before I had the chance to push myself up off the ground, he knelt down and helped me up.

"I'm so sorry. That was really clumsy of me," he said in a mortified tone.

He did look very upset. But he shouldn't have been, it was an accident. Besides, no one was hurt. Yet he looked apologetic.

"Oh, it's all right," I replied.

"Are you sure? Are you okay?" he asked.

Only after he'd asked me if I was okay did I realize that my hand was still in his. Gently I moved my hand away and stepped back. Guilt and embarrassment were clearly displayed on his face. Our eyes were locked together, two blazing stars gazing into each other.

Somehow, it really bothered me that he looked so upset. I didn't like to see the dullness in his eyes. It took away from the sparkle I imagined being there. He could have been beautiful. Maybe when he wasn't upset, he was gorgeous. There was life in him that I envied.

"I'm fine, thank you," I answered.

"Well, at least let me buy you a cup of coffee. I'm James Hamilton. What's your name?" he replied.

A small smile crept onto my lips. He was a human boy. If only he knew he was talking to an eighty-eight-year-old woman. I was old enough to be his great-grandmother. The only thing was, he saw me as a seventeen-year-old girl with light blue eyes and curly, midnight-black hair. But if he knew the truth, he'd be horrified. He looked like a sweet, innocent spirit. I was just about the last thing he'd ever need.

"Thank you, but I should be getting home. And it's Anne. Anne Emerson," I whispered.

Why had I told him my name? I wasn't sure. All I knew was that it had practically slid off of my tongue like water down a stream. It had happened before I knew it. And afterward, it left me in awe and confused.

Something warm was bubbling up within my chest. Like fire, it was comforting and terrifying. Part of me wanted to push it away, but another part said to let it spread. Of course, I had to try to be rational.

"You're sure you're all right?" James asked again.

He wore khaki pants and a sky blue button-up shirt. His blond hair was neatly combed to the side, giving me a marvelous view of his emerald eyes. Looking into them was like glimpsing a jungle. *He does have pretty eyes*, I thought. It was a romantic concept. The dark, brooding girl falls for the handsome, gentle boy. How ironic. It was slightly comical. He was cute and seemed so genuinely nice, but no. It wouldn't have even been worth trying.

"Yes, thank you," I replied.

He nodded. "Well, all right. It was nice meeting you."

His voice was tender, filled with peace. It was as if every word he spoke was a caramel candy. And his eyes, they were gems. Maybe he was a koala or even a fawn. Either way, he was too soft for me. Not in a bad way. I liked his gentleness. But I could break him, hurt him too easily. Emotionally and physically, that is.

I smiled. "It was nice meeting you, too."

Before I opened the door to step out into the warm summer air, Albert's eyes met mine. He raised an eyebrow while giving me a questioning glance. I turned away before he had the chance to come talk to me. A moment later, I was outside under the hot Savannah sun.

James was still present in my mind. I didn't want him to be, but I couldn't seem to get rid of him. Everything green I saw seemed to reflect his glimmering eyes. How was I going to change that? It was silly, anyway. I'd talked to him for only a minute or two—it wasn't much of anything. Interactions like that weren't particularly important. They were ordinary, bland things. It wasn't anything odd, so why was I still thinking about it?

I'd only walked for about five minutes when Albert caught up with me. I sighed as I heard him approaching.

What could possibly be wrong? He'd never come chasing after me before.

"You were flirting with that human boy," he said.

What? That wasn't what I had expected. This conversation was one of the last things I'd considered.

I stopped right where I was and turned around with my hands on my hips. "Excuse me?"

He tilted his head to the side. "You heard me."

I laughed in exasperation. "He knocked me over and helped me up. How exactly does that qualify as flirting?"

It was true. After all, we hadn't said anything to indicate attraction. Yes, I'd thought about it. But really, why did that matter? A number of boys had caught my attention over the years. I hadn't accepted them. Even so, it wasn't the first time I'd admired a man.

"The way you were looking into his eyes," Albert replied. "You like him."

What? No, that was impossible. He was cute, but that was all. I hadn't looked at him in a certain way. Had I? I mean, I'd been focused on him. And by that, I mean that maybe I'd gazed a bit too long into his alluring eyes. Still, I was allowed to feel attraction. That wasn't a crime. I could only do so much to avoid such things.

I rolled my eyes. "Okay, so he's cute."

Albert's eyes grew wide. "So, what I'm hearing is that I should bleach my hair and get contacts."

He was being overdramatic. Albert had hundreds

of girls—yes, literally hundreds—dreaming about him. If he'd advertised that he was lonely, they would have lined up on his doorstep. It would have been like people applying for a coveted job. He certainly didn't need me. I was one girl. Just one small girl. What was so special about me?

I crossed my arms. "Oh, don't be ridiculous."

"Anne, why a human boy? Why?" Albert whispered.

Was that what bothered him? He cared that the boy was human? Or maybe he cared that the boy was human and interested in me. Was he concerned with both?

"Why, what?" I replied.

"If you're going to fall for someone after seventy years of avoiding love, why does it have to be a human?" he asked in a sincerely questioning tone.

I took a step back. Why did he have to bring up my past like that? I didn't even know how so many people knew my story. Of course, it wasn't really a secret. I'd told people before. Not Albert, though. I just wasn't a fan of discussing it.

Besides, who said I was falling for James? Just because I'd thought he was cute didn't bring in any other aspects to the situation. Falling implied love. I certainly hadn't dropped my heart on the ground for James to pick up and walk off with. No, emotions like that simply didn't appear out of nothing. They had to grow, to be nurtured. Love built up, it didn't just occur. Even if you didn't know you were falling over a period of days, weeks, or months, it still took time.

I shook my head. "I'm not falling for anyone."

We stood there for a moment, simply staring at each other. His brown-black eyes bored into mine. I could see the intensity with which he was trying to come up with a response. This was one of the last conversations I would have ever dreamed of having.

What was this for? Why was he concerned? I suppose because he liked me. But after I'd rejected him on so many occasions, why was he still trying? It seemed like a waste of time. Why bother when so many women were eager to love you?

"Who are you trying to convince, Anne? You or me?" Albert asked.

I took another step back. He seriously believed what he was saying. Albert Jefferson was jealous. He was truly jealous. This day just kept getting stranger.

Never before had I considered the fact that men, or rather vampires like Albert, would become jealous of others. What reason did he have? Albert had more money, time, and even women than James. He couldn't possibly be comparing himself to a human boy. But if he was, what did that say?

I took a step toward him so that we were only a few inches apart, "I'm not trying to convince anyone of anything," I whispered.

It was true. I was too confused to be worrying

about fooling anyone. I didn't even know what was going on, so I didn't expect anyone else to either. It was a rather strange situation. I would have liked to know what was happening. But as I didn't, I could hardly go around trying to tell other people.

And even if I did know, Albert would not have been the first person on my list to inform. This really wasn't his business. He must have had other things to do.

"Sure, Anne. Sure," he replied before turning around and walking away.

I stood there in the middle of the sidewalk, watching him go. Incredible, I thought, absolutely incredible. He was going crazy if he actually thought I'd let myself fall for some human boy. No, I wouldn't do that. That would be a completely terrible idea. I mean, it couldn't end well. Could it? No, definitely not. It would go badly. That was for sure. Albert was just jealous that he'd seen another guy offer to do something nice for me. That was all there was to the whole thing. It was a very strange thing to be jealous of. After all, Albert could have offered to do the same.

But even so, I found myself standing there contemplating the situation. It wasn't as if I'd never heard of similar matches. They were rare, but they happened. Humans and vampires had fallen in love before. My sisters, Nina and Anya, were both dating wolves. Still, that was different from being with humans. The wolves…

well, they were similar to us. But humans, that was just so complicated.

Yet if I truly hadn't been considering the possibility of saying yes to him, why was I thinking so hard about it? If it was something I didn't intend to do, I had no need to concern myself with it. And clearly, I wasn't thinking of accepting. Because even if I did find him attractive, it could never lead to anything good. So no, I had no reason to worry about it. And even if some small part of me was slightly tempted, it would be better for him if I pretended like I wasn't.

Chapter 2
JUST A DANCE

The blaring music in the club made my ears want to bleed. It was just about the last place I wanted to be, but Nina and Anya had insisted I come. After refusing for three weeks, I'd gotten tired of saying no. But as I stood in the neon lights, I was highly regretting my decision. I looked like I belonged in this crowd about as much as a duck belonged in a family of kangaroos.

To almost any human, the room would have been entirely black. Not to me, though. I could see every single little detail of sparkling attire in the crowded room. Of course, I tried to ignore it. My senses were overwhelmed. Places like this weren't exactly where I found most of my enjoyment. I was only here for my sisters.

Nina, who was dancing with her boyfriend, Roy, glanced over at me. I smiled stiffly at her as she shook her head. A moment later, she made her way toward me.

"Why are you over here all by yourself? I didn't invite you out dancing so you could stand in the corner trying to blend into the walls," she said.

She should have known I would do exactly that. Who would I dance with? I didn't have a boyfriend, and I had no intention of marching out there to let some werewolf put his hands all over me. No, I was better off where I was.

"If you hadn't noticed, I'm a bit out of place," I mumbled.

The room was hot and uncomfortable. People were jammed together on the dance floor, practically running into each other. I didn't want to be a part of that.

She rolled her eyes. "Come on, Anne. Get with the times."

I pursed my lips. I wasn't particularly good at blending in.

Nina, who'd grown up in eighteenth-century India, hadn't had one bit of difficulty adapting through the decades. She'd cut her long, silky black hair so that it fell just below her shoulders and got a huge lotus flower tattooed on her back. Tonight she wore a tiny white skirt, lacy red top, and silvery stiletto ankle boots.

She was gorgeous. I'd always loved the way her hair framed her pretty face. Her nose was so cute, and her eyes were deep enough to be an ocean. She could have been a model.

"What about that guy over there? He's cute," she said while motioning toward a vamp on the far side of the room. Her eyes lit up as she glanced back at me.

He was tall with dark brown skin, creamy caramel eyes, and a thick beard. Obviously, he was a vampire. His clearly displayed fangs weren't leaving very much room open for debate about that. He looked maybe twenty-five. Of course, that meant absolutely nothing. He could have been born five hundred or thirty years ago. There was no way to tell.

A human girl with bleach-blonde hair wearing a skin-tight pink dress was standing beside him. His fangs were displayed right in front of her, but she was too drunk to tell. In the morning, she wouldn't remember any of it.

That was bad for her, but maybe good for him. She wouldn't remember his fangs, but who knew what else she'd forget about? I almost shivered at the thought. She'd probably come with some other girls. I hoped they'd find her soon and take her away. My chest grew tight; if they didn't find her, this could end very badly.

This was one of Albert's clubs. He owned an incredible number of businesses in Savannah, and other places, too. This was just one of his many venues. It wasn't vampire exclusive, though. Wolves and vamps filled the dance floor, but there were plenty of humans, too.

"I think he's occupied," I replied.

Before Nina had a chance to answer, another girl wearing black leather pants and a sheer midnight top approached him. Fangs slid out of her mouth as she pulled him away from the blonde and out onto the dance floor.

I released a sigh of relief. At least the human girl would make it out all right. That was what I was concerned with.

Nina frowned. "Well, you're hotter than her anyway. If I could get you to stop dressing like that, some guy might actually come over here to talk to you."

That hurt. But seriously, what was wrong with my clothes? I liked this dress. It actually fit me well. And personally, I thought it was very attractive.

I rolled my eyes. "Nina, I'm wearing a cocktail dress. What more do you want?"

She put her hands on her hips, "You didn't even wear the heels I set out for you."

I resisted the urge to gawk at her. Nina was such a wonderful sister; I loved her so much. But at times, she could be crazy. And her ideas about style—well, they were unique. I'd let her dress me once, and I'd come out of my room looking ridiculous. The dress made me feel like a giraffe, and the tights looked like a zebra. Looking at myself, I had thought I resembled a peacock. The whole attire had been absurd.

I frowned. "Yeah, because they were platform stilettos with spikes on them. You actually thought I'd walk out of the apartment in those?"

She sighed. "A girl can dream."

Anya, who was sitting at the bar with her boyfriend, Arthur, who happened to be Roy's older brother, waved to us. I smiled and waved back. Anya, who'd been born a native Cherokee, had adapted just as well as Nina. She wore a satin emerald jumpsuit with a pair of huge wedge heels. Her spiral curls fell like a waterfall all the way down her back. A moment later, Arthur turned around and grinned at us.

They were such a cute couple. I felt as if they belonged on a TV show. Arthur was only ever gentle when it came to Anya. Otherwise, he was fierce. But when he looked at her, it seemed as if he wanted to wrap her in his arms and never let go. What a wonderful love they had.

"You know," Nina began, "one day, I'm going to get you to go on a date even if it means I have to blindfold you and drag you there."

I smiled. "Well, when that day comes, be sure to let me know. I'll make every attempt to look as hideous as possible."

Nina knew I loved her. Her endless quest to marry me off would never cease. And so, I couldn't resist teasing her. After all, we'd spent decades together. It was truly like we were real sisters.

She laughed. "Just wait. One of these days, you'll fall in love."

Maybe, I thought. I looked around at all of the seemingly happy people packed into this tiny club. Purple, pink, and blue lights illuminated the room. Everywhere I looked, people were laughing, smiling, or dancing. They were all so incredibly carefree. There was a small part of me that wished I could be exactly like them.

"You should probably get back to Roy," I said. "He looks like he's uncomfortable."

It was true. Another vampire girl with short brown hair and a wicked smile was trying to get him to dance. Roy was holding his hands in the air and stepping backward. I resisted the urge to laugh. At least he was loyal. Nina deserved a guy like that.

Nina glanced over at him. "You're right. I'll take care of it."

She marched toward them with a determined look on her face. I almost felt bad for the poor girl. Making Nina angry was never a wise decision.

I leaned back against the wall, wishing I was anywhere else. When I closed my eyes, I imagined that I was sitting at home, wearing my pajamas, and watching *I Love Lucy*. That would have been so much better than this.

Moments later, I was pulled back to reality as the music halted. A man with a microphone stood on the small stage at the back of the room. The only good thing was that the music dulled as he began to speak.

He smiled at the crowd. "Hey! How's everybody doing tonight?"

The room erupted into cheers, clapping, and whistling.

"Well, your night is about to get better! The big man, the owner of this fine establishment, has just arrived." He stepped aside, allowing Albert space on the stage. "Ladies and gentlemen, Albert Jefferson!"

Many of the girls, human, wolf, and vampire, started screaming. He raised his drink in response. In the dim lights, it looked like wine. But everyone other than the humans knew better. One of the girls jumped up onto the stage, pulled him against her, and kissed him. He didn't even look shocked. As he kissed her, he wrapped one arm around her back and pulled her close.

I pursed my lips. "Incredible. Absolutely incredible," I grumbled.

After a few seconds more of shouting, the music was turned back up, and everything went back to normal. Anya's eyes met mine from across the room, and she winked at me. I smiled back. They all knew about Albert's seemingly never-ending attempts to convince me to go out with him. And unsurprisingly, they'd tried endless times to get me to accept. Well, what had just happened on that stage was exactly the reason I wouldn't go out with him. If he ever started acting like a rational individual, I might reconsider my response.

Even in the middle of the chaos, I was unable to ignore the fact that I was incredibly thirsty. I hadn't had anything to drink since last night, and it was starting to get to me. Hesitantly, I walked over to the bar. Anya and Arthur were still sipping their drinks. I slid onto a chair beside them.

The bartender, a wolf boy with glimmering gray eyes, walked over to stand in front of me. "What'll it be, gorgeous?"

"A v-regular," I replied.

He nodded, "Sure, babe."

Anya winked at me as he walked away. "You could say something to him, ya know."

Haha, so funny. He wasn't really my type. I barely even noticed him as he walked away to pour my glass.

"I just did," I replied.

She laughed, letting her fangs slip out from behind her lips, "You know what I mean."

I did. But no, that wasn't going to happen. I simply didn't want him.

He walked back over toward me, carrying a tall glass, "Here you go."

I nodded. "Thank you."

I kept my eyes on my glass, hoping he would walk away. Maybe if I ignored him, he'd go. I didn't want to meet his eyes. If I did, he might think I wanted him to stay.

He grinned. "You know, that stuff's been in the fridge for a few weeks now. Is there any chance I could get you something more fresh?"

He tilted his neck to the side to reveal two puncture marks. It wasn't uncommon for vampires to bite their partners. It gave both people a rush. And since we could control when we released our venom, there wasn't any risk of someone being accidentally turned. It was intoxicating.

Before I had a chance to respond, Albert cut in. "Thanks for the offer, bud, but she'll be passing on that."

The boy's face turned red with embarrassment as he quickly moved away and walked to the other side of the bar. I gave a small sigh of relief, but that faded just as soon as Albert turned to face me.

A small grin crept onto his face. "So, Ms. Emerson, you're not Amish after all."

I bit my lip, turning my face away from his. All I wanted was to sip my drink in peace, but everyone seemed determined to prevent me from doing it.

"I'm beginning to think you're stalking me," I mumbled.

He laughed. "You're the one in my club, remember?" His voice was melodious.

I sighed in resignation; he did have a point.

He leaned closer to me. "Look, it's a Saturday night. We've both had a long week. How about you give me a dance? Just one little dance?"

Anya elbowed me hard in the side. I glanced over my shoulder and gave her a dirty look. Say yes, she mouthed. I pursed my lips before glancing down at my drink. And as I sat there staring into my glass, something otherworldly must have happened because as I looked back at Albert, I said, "Yes."

He sat there for a moment, simply staring at me. "Did you just say yes?"

I nodded. We both seemed to be in shock at the words that had just escaped from my mouth. What was I supposed to do now?

As we stood up, he took my hand and led me out onto the middle of the dance floor. I had absolutely no idea what I was doing or why I was doing it, but it was too late to turn back now. After we'd made it to the middle of the room, he put his hands on my waist and pulled me close to him. Nina, who happened to be standing only a few feet away, looked over at us in utter shock. A moment later, she grinned and gave me a thumbs up.

Albert's face was dangerously close to mine. Strategically, I turned my face away from his to look over toward the stage. That wasn't something I was ready for.

He rubbed his thumb across my hipbone. "Tell me, Anne. Has it been seventy years since you've kissed anyone?"

I almost froze. The question should have been expected, but I hadn't thought of it. A dance was rarely ever just a dance. I should have known that.

"Why does it matter?" I asked.

My voice was a little shaky, but it was firm. I didn't want to seem helpless. One of the last things I wanted was for him to see me as a little girl.

He chuckled before replying, "I suppose that's a yes."

He'd guessed correctly. I hadn't kissed anyone since Glen. No one felt right. Handsome, yes. But right? No. The idea of kissing someone I couldn't love was almost repulsive. If there was no connection, why would I bother?

We fell into silence for a few moments. I was trying to ignore the fact that this wasn't half as bad as I'd expected it to be. Really, it wasn't miserable at all. The scent of his cologne made me feel warm and lightheaded. There was some sort of a quivering feeling in my abdomen. I hadn't felt anything like it for so long.

All of a sudden, I found myself turning my lips toward his. A few seconds later, our mouths collided.

In a burst of passion, he pulled us together and tangled his hands in my hair. It was electric. After being alone for so long, my body was attempting to drink up as much of his touch as I possibly could.

It made no sense, but I tried not to think about it. If I focused too hard on how strange this all was, I might risk ruining it. This feeling spreading through my stomach was too marvelous.

Somehow, we ended in a secluded area separated from the rest of the club by a thin curtain. As we kissed, I let him lift me up into the air. His unearthly strength held me up as I ran my hands through his soft hair. Albert's brown curls separated between my fingers, coating my hands in a coffee-colored curtain.

In the dark, hot room, time and space seemed to

be suspended. We fell into a world of our own where we were both anxious and desperate for love. Never in my wildest dreams had I imagined I'd be relying on Albert for what I'd been subconsciously wanting for so long. I wanted to be loved. After all, seventy years was a very long time to be alone.

"Anne," he whispered.

Albert's strong arms wrapped around my back. His body was stone against my own marble form. But we couldn't crush each other because we were both so immortally strong. Our lips were just as hard.

"Yes," I mumbled into his neck.

Why was this so good? How had we even gotten here? It didn't even matter. We were in this moment, and that was the important thing. Albert was still Albert, and I was still me, but I needed this — we both did.

"You're perfect," he replied.

Did he really think I was perfect? What if he thought I was beautiful, too? So many things could change. Was any of this worth the risk?

Gently he brushed my hair off my shoulder and kissed my neck. His fangs pierced my skin. My body shuddered. I fell against him as his teeth sunk deeper into my neck. For a moment, it was blissful. I could feel the sweet sensation that always came with a bite. It was like flying, like walking on clouds. I wanted to sink into it. Perhaps this was what gold would have tasted like.

But then, I was sucked back into another time and

place when I'd first felt the sting of a different man's fangs upon my neck.

I was transported back to the dark alley with Glen's body on the ground below me. The dark figure's fangs sank deep into my skin. As he drained my body, I felt all pain and anxiety vanish from my mind. It was like falling into a peaceful sleep. Slowly, my eyes closed as I lost all consciousness.

A moment later, searing pain enveloped my body in absolute agony. I felt every inch of torment as his venom spread through my veins. I was no longer in the dark alley outside the dancehall but rather in the middle of the woods underneath a tall sycamore tree. I desperately wanted to cry out, but my lips seemed glued shut.

"You'll make for a beautiful immortal," the vampire, a man with deep blue eyes and wavy mahogany hair, whispered.

I was frozen in pain and fear. This was the man who had taken my life away. He was the reason I was in undesirable pain. He had murdered the love of my life right before my eyes. Again, I drifted into a dreamless sleep.

What could have been hours, days, or weeks later, I awoke with a sense of power flowing through my blood. As I examined my surroundings, my heightened senses overwhelmed my newly immortal brain. I could see every blade of grass, speck of dirt, and inch of bark. The sounds of the forest were a melody more gorgeous than I'd ever been able to comprehend before. And as I looked at the sky, I could examine each individual star. And yet none of this comforted me nearly enough to distract from the aching sensation in my throat.

"You're just as incredible as I predicted," he whispered in a sultry tone.

I turned to him, anger bubbling up within me. This was the man who had taken everything from me. He'd stolen my love, my mortality, and my world. Everything I'd ever loved, he'd ripped away from me for his sick amusement. My fangs burst from my mouth in fury.

He smiled at me. "You're thirsty."

"You have no idea," I whispered. But I wasn't craving blood. I was craving revenge.

Less than a second later, I'd shoved him to the ground. He looked up at me with total shock in his eyes, but before he had a chance to respond, I sunk my teeth into his throat. On that night, I had killed my murderer.

As I opened my eyes, I came back to the twenty-first century. Half a moment later, I shoved Albert away. His eyes met mine in confusion; he was entirely perplexed.

"What did I do?" Albert asked.

It was as if I could still feel every bit of pain I'd experienced that terrible night. My body was flooded with fear.

"I just can't," I whispered before turning away from him and leaving the room.

I burst through the door and out into the brisk evening air. Dizziness consumed me as I ran down the sidewalk. Everything seemed to sway from side to side. My heels clattered as I sprinted away from the club, Albert, and my immortal reality.

I ran, ran, and ran until I once again found myself in a dark, nightmarish alley. As my head spun from the memory of the agony, I collapsed onto the cold, wet concrete.

Chapter 3
PRETEND

It had been less than forty-eight hours since I'd last seen him when Albert made his Monday morning trip to the café. He didn't look too good. His hair fell sloppily in front of his eyes, and he was absent a tie. The top button of his black dress shirt wasn't buttoned, making him look slightly disheveled. Not surprisingly, that made the other waitresses swoon even more. I would have gladly let one of them give him his drink, but he refused to accept it from anyone but me.

I hadn't told anyone what had transpired Saturday night in the back of the club. Long before Nina and Anya had arrived home, I'd cleaned up and changed into a fresh pair of linen pajamas. Even though I hadn't slept in seventy years, the relaxation that normal evenings brought was reason enough to wear the soft, comfortable attire. When Nina and Anya had come bursting through the door with huge smiles on their faces, I plastered a fake look of contentment on my own. Of course, they'd interrogated me about the whole situation. But I hadn't told them any more than I would have revealed to anyone else. He'd asked me to dance, and I'd said yes. That was all there was to it.

So today, life was back to normal. I would pretend that it had all been a very strange dream. That would be almost enough to keep it off my mind.

I set Albert's drink in front of him with a blank expression on my face. It was just a normal day. There was no reason to act any differently. Of course, trying to brainwash myself into forgetting the events of that evening didn't take away from the heavy feeling in my abdomen. I couldn't seem to shake it. The fluttering sensation was persistent, though I tried to pretend it wasn't there.

He looked up at me. "Anne, about Saturday night...."

Oh no, he was going to bring it up. It seemed as if a lump was stuck in my throat. Why was this happening? I didn't want to feel this way.

"There's nothing to talk about," I interrupted. "After all, it was just a dance."

Maybe I could talk myself into it. But somehow, I doubted I'd be able to do the same with him. Even if I could get him to stop talking, he wouldn't forget about it.

He nodded, seemingly accepting the situation for what it was.

He sat in his usual booth for far longer than normal.

Staring at the table, Albert looked miserable. I felt a bit guilty, but I couldn't bring myself to approach him. It was all too heavy. If I talked to him, there was no way I'd be able to eliminate the butterflies in my stomach. It was hard enough for me to admit the annoying sensation. I certainly didn't want to encourage it.

After drinking three of his usuals, he simply sat there staring at his hands. He looked...well, awful. But that didn't change anything. It had been a dance, that was all.

About an hour later, the bell on the front door chimed as a customer walked in. I left the kitchen to take his order. But when I reached the main seating area, I saw the last person I had expected to see.

James stood in front of me with a dozen red roses in his hand. My jaw literally dropped as his eyes met mine. I was stunned speechless. How? Why? This was slightly crazy.

He smiled down at me. "Anne, I was hoping you'd be here. These are for you."

James handed me the flowers with a huge grin on his face. I accepted them with a look of astonishment clearly displayed on my own. What exactly was I supposed to say? The gesture was so romantic. He was such a gentleman.

"I was hoping, maybe, if it sounds all right to you, you'd go out with me sometime?" James asked sheepishly.

It was almost as if I was in a dream. I had imagined this scenario in my head. Of course, I had never planned on it coming true. Now it was real, and I didn't really know how I was supposed to react.

I was awkwardly silent for far too long before finally figuring out what to say. "Uh, sure."

Wait, what? I'd just said yes. Had I even intended to do that? I wasn't sure. Either way, it had certainly happened.

He smiled brightly. "Wow, yes! I mean, that's awesome. Great! Can I pick you up tomorrow after work?"

He was so sweet, almost to the point where I wanted to melt in his arms. How was he so nice? I'd never met a boy like this, not since Glen. And, in truth, it made me all the more attracted to him.

I nodded. "I get off at six."

He grinned as wide as a little kid in a candy store. "Awesome. I'll, uh, see you then."

That smile made my heart seem to bounce. Of course, that was impossible, considering my heart was frozen forever. But still, the sensation was the same.

Before turning around, James smiled at me once more. On his way out the door, he waved back at me. I gave a small smile in response. For several more moments, I stood there staring down at the roses in my hands. What had just happened?

I didn't realize Albert had witnessed the whole

encounter until I turned around. He looked like a wounded animal. We both stood there in silence, simply looking at each other. His deep eyes were filled with sadness. It made me feel a little sick. I'd caused that pain in his eyes. That had never been my intention.

He pursed his lips. "And to think I actually thought I'd started to figure you out." His voice was almost bitter sounding.

I shook my head. "It's not like that, Albert."

Of course, I could hardly believe myself. He didn't seem to buy my response. I didn't blame him. After all, this situation resembled a novel. It was practically unbelievable. Then again, love triangles were certainly real. They occurred more often than people liked to admit. The reality was that it was rare for two people to love each other with the same intensity. In most cases, one person was far more infatuated. But Albert could not have been in love with me, could he?

He laughed sardonically before replying, "Really?"

Albert was getting angry. It scared me a little. I didn't want this to be a confrontation. In reality, I hadn't technically done anything wrong. Even so, I felt sick.

I frowned. "You wouldn't understand."

That was true. He'd been with so many girls that I doubted he was capable of true attachment. What he had for me was a fleeting desire. Then again, it had lasted for years.

He crossed his arms over his chest. "Oh, really?

Enlighten me as to why not."

He wouldn't be happy if I told him the truth. Did anyone want to see themself as flighty? Probably not. We all had some inward desire to be loyal, or at least I did. Maybe I was naïve.

"You don't know the first thing about love," I hissed.

He couldn't have, right? All of his romances were so brief that he never had time to form an emotional connection. To him, it was all physical. Albert wasn't the type of man to fall in love.

His eyes turned dark. "You know nothing about me. Don't pretend you do."

There was a chance he was right, but I'd watched him for years. Even he didn't seem to remember all the girls he'd broken. Perhaps they didn't even have faces to him. Of course, I'd always observed from the outside. But with people — vampires — like him, you could usually tell. But even so, there was no way for me to see what was going through his head. He'd never told me his thoughts about women. Then again, why would he?

I looked directly into his stormy eyes, "You're right. We know nothing about each other."

And with one final, furious glance in my direction, he stormed out the front door. I watched him go, still holding the roses in my hands. With no customers in the dining area and everyone else back in the kitchen, I was left utterly alone.

What had I done? I'd just agreed to go out with a human. How could I have been so incredibly stupid? I had acted like a naïve, human teenage girl. It was completely ridiculous. There was no way anything good could possibly come from it. But how could I have refused him? His emerald eyes had been so full of hope. And after I'd said yes, they had lit up like sparkling jewels. He was so sweet, so innocent, so kind. There was no way I could hurt him. Breaking his heart would be the cruelest thing I'd ever done.

But going out with a human, that had to be crossing some sort of line. Would it have been better to have disappointed him? In the long run, probably so. But in the moment when I would have had to see the sadness I'd caused him, absolutely not. That would be too painful for either of us. Still, I had no clue what I was doing. How was this even supposed to work? What did I do? There wasn't exactly a manual for this sort of thing. I couldn't call 1-800-VAMPIRE and ask what to do. For this, I was entirely on my own.

How would this end? Most likely in some painful disaster. Would both of us be hurt? Definitely. But was it worth it? I had no idea, but I couldn't go ask his opinion on the topic. In his mind, all he'd done was ask a cute waitress on a date. There was nothing unnatural about that. He'd acted completely rationally. I was the one who'd done something stupid.

Yet if I had to do it over again, I wouldn't have

changed a thing. I wanted to be loved. For seventy years, I'd watched people throw it away. They took for granted the human affection that I so desperately craved. To be a mortal again would have been almost heavenly. I would have given pretty much anything to feel my heartbeat for a few more moments.

But with James, maybe I could find some small bit of happiness. I didn't want anything extraordinary, no diamond rings or gold. I simply wanted to feel content. Even if I couldn't be truly happy, I would have settled for contentment. That would have been enough.

A small bit of peace was all I wanted. I had thought that putting a stake in the heart of the vampire who'd turned me would bring satisfaction to my soul. But when I'd looked into his lifeless eyes, all I had felt was contempt. Not even taking his own immortal existence had brought me any type of release in my own. Because no matter how agonizing I made his death, it would have never given me my mortality back. Love wasn't the only thing that had evaded me for seventy years. Peace had as well.

When I'd kissed Albert, it had given me a rush. After being alone for so long, kissing almost anyone would have felt right. But no, there was no way we'd actually had any chemistry. We were just too different. Had I imagined the butterflies? Maybe. But still, the continual pressure in my abdomen was too hard to ignore. A girl like me had no place in his life. I'd been starved for affection, so yes, it had felt good. But it had all been out of desperation. I simply couldn't allow my base impulses to control me like that. All he would ever see me as was a pretty face. I wouldn't settle for being used.

But kissing him had awoken something within me. A desire for love and affection had been rekindled within my soul. A spark had been lit that had started a fire within my heart.

Chapter 4

CRUEL TEMPTATIONS

We were walking side-by-side along the beach. Every so often, the tide would rush in and cover our bare feet. I loved the sand between my toes and the salty water flooding over my ankles. Even though I had so many awful memories, I could never leave my hometown. Georgia was where my heart was planted.

My long sundress danced in the wind as the salty ocean breeze blew around us. Every time I took a step, my feet sank into the soft, warm sand. It was so relaxing. Looking out onto the horizon gave me a sense of hope, and what a wonderful feeling that was.

I'd been silent for most of the walk, listening to stories from his senior year. James had graduated in the spring but still hadn't figured out what he wanted to do. I listened intently as he told me about himself. Several times he'd stopped to ask me questions, but I'd always redirected the conversation back to him. The last thing I wanted to talk about was myself. Besides, his life was so fascinating. I always found humans interesting, especially ones as special as James.

When the sun started to set, we sat on the sand to watch it make its descent. He was incredibly close to me. I was acutely aware of every breath I took. Every single one of his heartbeats was like a soft, gentle thud. He was so…human. Not that that was a bad thing. On the contrary, it was lovely. Mortality was such a gift.

"So, what are your ex's like?" James asked in a casual tone.

It wasn't an odd question. But how was I supposed to answer it?

I looked out at the ocean. There had been a time, seventy-or-so years ago when I'd sat on this very same beach. Back then, I'd looked out at the waves, knowing that so many men were across the ocean dying for our freedom. Glen had sat with me, wishing he was over there with them. But I had been glad he wasn't. We'd known each other since childhood, and I'd loved him since the first day I saw him. When I turned sixteen, and he took me out for the first time, I thought to myself, This is the man I'm going to marry.

"Normal, I guess," I replied in a soft voice. "I only have one."

James raised his eyebrows. "Only one?"

It was rather surprising. At the rate modern teenagers dated, I should have had at least a few more. But no, where I was from, it was entirely normal.

I gave him a soft smile. "Only one."

"I feel really bad now," he laughed.

I tilted my head to the side. "Why?"

He had no reason to feel guilty. Falling in love wasn't a crime. James was so sweet that I could only wonder why a girl would ever leave him. I doubted James was even capable of abandoning a woman. He was too genuinely kind.

He shook his head, looking out toward the sun. "I've been with a few more people than you."

I could hardly believe he thought of himself as the lesser being in this. If either one of us was corrupting the other, I was the one in the wrong. There was no way he could paint himself as stealing anything from me, certainly not my innocence. After all, I'd killed the vampire who'd changed me. I had literally obliterated a man. All he'd done was have his heart broken.

"Doesn't matter," I replied.

We fell into silence for a few moments. "So this guy, were the two of you serious?"

A deep sadness fell over me. Had we been serious? Of course. I'd been so close to being married. My dreams had almost been fulfilled. Those sweet babies I'd dreamed of, they'd never exist. I'd never carry a child within me, never have the chance to nurture a baby with my body. It broke my heart.

I ran my fingertips through the soft sand. "About as serious as you can be."

He nodded. "I'm sorry."

What? Why would he be sorry? That didn't make much sense at all.

I looked at him with curiosity. "Why?"

His eyes met mine. "Because you lost him."

I sat there, simply staring at him. Our eyes seemed to be locked together. We were trying to discover who the other was and how much it mattered. Of course, he'd never guess the truth about me. But maybe I could find the truth about him. What he'd said was so heartfelt.

"I suppose it's too late to do anything about that," I whispered.

Very, very late. I'd attended Glen's funeral, standing in the very back with a dark veil over my face. No one knew what had happened to me. They'd thought that maybe I'd been kidnapped or perhaps murdered in another gruesome way. My poor parents had never received any closure.

He moved closer to me. "Maybe I can make it hurt a little less."

A moment later, his lips were on mine. It didn't feel anything like kissing Albert. James's lips were soft and sweet. I could feel the humanity in them. Albert's were hard, firm, and cold. Of course, it wasn't his fault. Our immortal forms were made as hard as stone. There was nothing soft about us.

With James, I had to be so incredibly careful. If I moved too quickly or too hard, I could literally break him. I had to treat him as a flower whose petals were as soft as a feather. My movements had to be lessened to practically nothing. Hurting him would feel like a crime. The last sliver of humanity I had within me would burst into oblivion.

Moments later, he wrapped his arms around my waist. I became entirely motionless, but he didn't seem to notice. He kept coming closer and closer until we were pressed against each other.

All of a sudden, my senses erupted in a burst of color. All I was aware of was the bright blood streaming through his veins. I could smell it, taste it, and feel its very presence. It was the one thing I wanted. Its sweet aroma was practically intoxicating. There was nothing more important than the burning sensation in my throat.

It had been a very long time since I'd felt such a powerful sensation. I always kept myself fed to avoid even the smallest bits of temptation. Lamb, calf, and deer's blood were the most filling. The more I drank, the fewer urges I had toward humans. But before I'd learned to control the newfound needs of my immortal existence, I'd been familiar with this temptation. In the ten years between my rebirth and stabilization, I'd fed from humans. Even then, I'd been selective. My victims had been the lowlifes of society; drug dealers, thieves, and human traffickers. Innocents had never been my targets. Even though I'd been in a crazed, animal-like state, I'd had some semblance of morality.

Then, I met Nina. She'd been living her immortal life at a higher standard for hundreds of years. With time, she weaned me from my lust for human blood and brought me to a new, enlightened perspective of reality. Soon after, Anya joined us. She'd already found her own way to an animal-only diet. Independently, we'd been lost, lonely, and scared. Together, we'd created our own coven, our own family.

But when I inhaled the sweet scent of James's blood, the warmth of his skin, and the freshness of his breath, everything came flooding back. I remembered the unique, intoxicating taste of human blood. It wasn't like animal blood, which I consumed begrudgingly out of pure necessity — it was a drug. But like an addict, even though I'd been clean for decades, the urge would always come back. It was the most sickening burden of our kind. We craved the unique thrill that came from human blood, yet most of us worked intensely hard to resist it.

Even Albert, who enjoyed many vices, had never been known to drink human blood. Everyone in his abnormally large coven was held to just as high a standard. Any enlightened children of the night, with even a shallow sense of decency, refused to give in to such animalistic impulses. That is unless they were given permission. Relationships between vampires and werewolves were common, and so was consensual feeding. Even other romantically involved vampires would feed from each other.

As James kissed me, I tried to fight the urge. I wanted to enjoy the gentle, innocent kiss. It was soft, peaceful, and nothing more. There should have been absolutely nothing complicated about this. But even though I tried to push it from my mind, it overwhelmed me.

I felt my fangs begin to extend from my mouth. But before they punctured him, I threw myself backward. I landed with a soft thud on the warm sand. Relief flooded through me as I realized just how terribly that kiss could have ended. If I'd let him touch me for even seconds longer, I would have lost control. I would have killed him. Within moments, I could have taken his life.

The worst part was, he would have enjoyed it. Venom gave everyone, vamps included, a sense of bliss that nothing could match. Once it dispersed itself into your bloodstream, it was impossible to stop. You'd be immersed in pleasure until you became too buzzed to know what was happening.

He looked at me with confusion spread across his face. I could only imagine what he was thinking. But nothing mattered other than the terrifying fact that I could have taken his life only moments before. That would have been an atrocity that I'd never be able to forgive myself for.

His eyes held intense guilt. "Anne, I'm sorry. I thought you wanted it. Did I do something wrong?"

I shook my head. "You didn't do anything. I just

feel sick."

I stood up, brushing the sand off myself. The only thing I could do was run. My throat was throbbing. It was as if a fire was coursing through my body. I could hardly imagine a more agonizing sensation. I was choking on flames. My body had become predatory, but I had to rely on my self-control to stop myself before I went any farther.

Why had I ever thought this would work? It had been such a stupid decision from the start. There was no way we could have actually had a relationship. And if we'd started one, he would have ended up dead. Thinking that this could have actually worked had been a delusion, a fairytale. But this wasn't some Hallmark movie; it didn't end with the prince saving the princess. He couldn't change what I was. No matter how badly I wanted to be mortal, I could never be human again. In this nightmare, the princess would have killed the prince.

"I'll go with you," James replied.

I bit my lip. "No, no, I'll be fine."

He reached for my hand, but I stepped backward. If I was around him for much longer, I wouldn't be able to control myself. Once I'd caught the scent, I could only contain my urges for so long. Each time I spoke, it was like breathing fire. The flames were beginning to consume me.

"I can't just let you go alone," he said.

I turned to look at him with anger in my eyes.

At this point, it didn't matter if I hurt him emotionally. The only important thing was getting myself away from him before he ended up dead. It was as if I'd swallowed burning charcoal.

"I'm leaving," I whispered in a tone that seemed to terrify him.

He glanced out at the ocean for just a moment. But before he had a chance to look back at me, I disappeared.

I ran until I was probably miles away from him. Eventually, his scent began to fade. But the memory of what I'd almost done was still at the front of my mind. Sitting on that beach, I could have killed him. He would have died, and it all would have been my fault. If I'd had one bit of common sense, I'd have never gone anywhere alone with him. He deserved so much better than me; I was a monster.

I was a creature of nightmares. When humans feared the darkness for unspoken reasons, it was because of creatures like me. There was something perverse and sick about my very existence. No matter how hard I tried, I'd never be able to make up for all of the pain I'd caused.

As I wandered through the woods, memories of horror flooded through my mind. I'd haunted the slums of Savannah. One particularly vile night, I'd run into a drunken man attacking a teenage girl. She'd looked over at me, her eyes pleading for help. It had only taken me an instant to snap his throat. Within moments, I'd drained the blood from his body. I had hoped she'd be relieved.

After all, I'd saved her life. But when her eyes had met mine, the only thing displayed within them had been terror. She had fallen backward, too terrified to scream. As I had looked down at myself, I'd seen blood splattered all over my dress.

Later that night, Nina had found me curled up in a ball in a wet, dark alley. She'd been so gorgeous in her bright yellow, Jackie Kennedy style dress. When she knelt down next to me and wiped the blood from my lips with her cream-colored handkerchief, our eyes locked for the first time. In that moment, she'd saved my life.

But as the years passed, I could never forget the fear in that girl's eyes when she'd seen what I truly was. I was a monster, a killer. The memory of her terror and disgust would live in my mind forever.

Standing in the middle of the woods, I found myself reluctant to go home. After all, what would I say? Nina and Anya had both been so excited for me. They'd been begging me to go out with someone for years. But when I went back to the apartment, I'd have nothing good to tell them. How had they even expected me to control myself around a human? Maybe they were just better, stronger than me. Evidently, they could handle themselves perfectly well when tempted with mortal blood. Still, Roy and Arthur's necks were decorated with an array of puncture marks. Their long, blond hair was enough to cover the scars from humans. But among the wolves, everyone knew what they were from. I had no opinion on the matter. It really wasn't any of my business. They knew exactly what they were getting into.

Neither of the girls had ever mentioned it to me, but I suspected both Arthur and Roy had requested to be turned. After all, wolves aged just like humans. In a few more years, the difference in their apparent ages would draw too much attention from humans. It would have to happen soon, but Nina and Anya were probably just trying to put it off.

Part of me wished I could have a love like that. It would be so easy. When I had the uncontrollable urge to feed, he'd be right there, ready and willing. I'd take just enough to satisfy myself and give him a blissful rush. With a wolf, it was one thing. They had been born into our world. I wouldn't have felt bad about it. And they were capable of defending themselves. But with a human, I wouldn't have been able to shake the constant feeling of guilt.

As the stars began to peek out from behind the clouds, I sat down on the soft forest floor. I rested my back against an oak tree before tilting my head up toward the sky. Tonight, I would imagine things were different. I could pretend that when I went home, everything would be all right. That maybe when the sun rose in the morning, I'd be human again. Well, it was nice to dream.

Chapter 5
YOU'RE A...

My interactions with Albert still hadn't gone back to normal. Every morning he tried to make eye contact with me. I just didn't have the energy for it. But really, how much longer could we go on like this?

Each time I felt his gaze upon my skin, I felt heat course through me. A sense of uneasiness flooded my being. It only took a glance for him to throw me off balance. How was he capable of that? There was just something about him.

"Anne," he whispered as I set his drink in front of him.

I sighed; at some point, I'd probably have to acknowledge his existence. Not that I hadn't been thinking about him, I had. He was impossible to ignore. When he'd kissed me on that unforgettable night, I'd fallen into a glorious bliss. It hadn't been the same as the thrill from the venom, but it had been pretty close. He'd held me like he knew exactly what he was doing. There hadn't been any hesitancy in his actions. But when his fangs had moved to my neck, he'd crossed a line.

What would have happened if he hadn't bitten me, though? Would I have gone home with him? Would I have taken him back to the apartment? It could have changed everything. But did I seriously want to think about that?

"Yes," I replied.

He looked up at me in shock. "Could we talk about what happened?"

There was a lump in my throat. Soon after, the butterflies returned. I simply couldn't seem to get rid of them. Albert Jefferson unraveled me.

My eyes met his. "Is there really any reason to?"

He raised his eyebrows. "I mean, I think so."

Was there any way to resist this man? His luscious voice seemed as silky as buttermilk. This was why women found it so hard to walk away from him.

I bit my lip before sliding into the booth across from his demanding stare. He smiled softly at me, a glimmer of mischief shining in his eyes. Albert seemed to be waiting for me to speak, but I pursed my lips instead.

He took a sip of his drink. "First, I'd like to say that I thoroughly enjoyed our little liaison. And if I'm being honest, I know you did too." He stopped for a moment, seemingly waiting for me to respond. When I simply kept staring at him, he decided to continue. He leaned closer to me before speaking. "So, if you don't mind me asking, what was it that made you run away?"

I didn't really want to tell him, but before I had a chance to stop myself, the words just came flooding out. "You bit me."

I said it like an accusation. I hadn't wanted his fangs to touch me. But even so, I'd never communicated that. In truth, I hadn't imagined that he would bite me. It seemed like such a vague concept; the thought hadn't crossed my mind.

Confusion spread across his face. "You got upset because I bit you?"

I nodded. Why did this confuse him so much? Was I really the only person that it bothered? As he moved to take another sip, his hair brushed to the side. I caught a short glimpse of his neck, only to see that it was covered in bite marks. I looked down at the table, sighing.

"So," he began, "if I agreed not to bite you, could we pick up where we left off? That is if you're not too busy playing with that human boy."

That stung. He referred to James as if he were no more than an insect. Maybe it didn't have anything to do with him being human, though. It could have just been out of jealousy, or maybe annoyance. Even so, he didn't have any business knowing how I felt about James. It wasn't something I wanted him to be concerned with.

I rolled my eyes. "I don't know, Albert. We don't really fit well together."

My statement had been honest. We were polar

opposites. It would have been like trying to blend fire and water. Was there even really a point?

He grinned before replying, "That didn't seem to concern you very much before."

Had I been crazy before, or was I just being cautious now? He seemed to think the latter. I wasn't sure of my opinion on the subject.

I bit my lip. "I don't know."

He took my hand and pulled me up onto my feet. A moment later, he grabbed my waist and pulled me against him.

"What are you doing?!" I whispered.

His chest was pressed against mine. I shivered as his strong hands gripped my hips. The butterflies were no longer a subtle sensation—they'd transformed into full-fledged pellets plummeting inside me. I felt sick but excited. Anxious, yet filled with anticipation.

"Convincing you," he replied.

His lips met mine as his hands came up to stroke my hair. After a few moments, I relaxed. His right hand was tangled in my curls while his left was wrapped around me. I reached up to stroke his neck. As my fingers traced his skin, I could feel a trail of bite marks. The thought of another vampire touching him like that made me want to hold him tighter.

"You're my little dove," he whispered in a gentle tone.

I rested my head against his chest. It really was

nice just to feel someone's arms around me and not have the urge to kill them. I could smell his cologne without my throat catching on fire, rest my head near his neck without wanting to sink my fangs into him, and taste his lips without being tempted by his blood. Yes, vamps bit each other. And yes, they enjoyed it. But it wasn't an uncontrollable urge. It was nice to do, yet it took very little effort to resist.

This was enjoyable, almost freeing. I let him hold me, not wanting to worry about what it meant. Feeling his arms around me was enough.

"Come home with me, take the rest of the day off," he urged.

I laughed. "Somehow, I think that's probably a bad idea."

He tilted his head to the side. "Why?"

I laughed. "I'm not going to just walk into your nest like some sort of trophy."

All those vampire girls in his coven would look at me with hate in their eyes. The very thought of that terrified me. Women could be vicious, especially when it came to partners.

He touched my cheek. "No one would see it like that."

Yes, they would. There was more that I wasn't telling him, though. I couldn't just go home with him when thoughts of James were still plaguing my mind. There was no reason to think of him. After all, he was far better off away from me. Still, it was hard to just forget someone like that. James was special. He wasn't arrogant or self-absorbed. In many ways, he reminded me of Glen. Albert was…well, a less reputable sort of man. But even so, he'd been pursuing me for years now. And honestly, I was starting to enjoy the attention.

I smiled sarcastically. "Well, that's exactly the type of thing I'd expect from you, Romeo. How many girls have you taken back there with you anyway?"

We both had teasing looks in our eyes. This had turned playful. There was something intrinsic about what was happening. Age-old relations between men and women were playing a huge role in our conversation. Flirting was an art, and vampires were just as good at it as humans. As long as he didn't bite me, I'd be fine. The rest of it didn't matter.

He smirked before replying, "We probably shouldn't talk about that."

I raised my eyebrows. "So, you won't tell me?"

He shrugged. "I mean, I can. I'm just not sure it would be a particularly productive conversation. I still say we head back to my place. No one would bother us there. We could just get drinks and talk if that's all you want."

Why was his offer so tempting? Since things really weren't going to work out with James, and Albert did seem like he was making a genuine effort, was it really a bad idea? After all, what harm could a couple of drinks do? Nina and Anya would be so excited for me.

His tempting lips were so hard to ignore. I could use this relaxation. I'd been so tense, so stressed. It would be good to let loose.

"Well, okay. But we'll only have a few drinks and talk. That's it, got it?" I asked.

He nodded with a huge grin on his face. "Deal."

I untied my apron from around my waist. "Let me just go put this in the kitchen and grab my bag."

Adjusting my hair was a very hard thing to do when the only mirror I had was the back of a giant pot. It looked decent, but nothing more. I wished it would have been better. My hair was simply hard to contain.

Albert lived in the penthouse of a giant apartment building that he'd converted into a huge den for Savannah's vampire population. Vamps moved from all over the world to join his coven. He was rich, popular, and connected. So when I walked through the front door, dozens of eyes would fall on me. I'd never actually been there, but Nina and Anya had. They'd told me how gorgeous it was. It was supposedly like a never-ending, high-class party. I was wearing a plain green dress, pumps, and a cardigan. Well, it would have to do. My curls were a little frizzy, but that was normal. I looked about as good as I was going to get.

Before walking back out to Albert, I took a sip from my "water bottle." I always tried to have emergency blood with me, just in case. Just as I was about to fasten the lid back on, the kitchen door opened. I looked up, expecting to see Albert. But instead, James was standing in the doorway. In shock, I dropped my bottle. A moment later, there was blood splattered all over the floor.

I didn't know what to do, so I froze. There was no way this would end well. He'd seen the blood; he knew what I was. I couldn't hide it anymore.

It took James a few seconds, but eventually, he said, "Is that...blood?"

I bit my lip; there was literally no way to play this off. "Um, yes."

His jaw dropped. "You're—you're a vampire."

We stood there in silence until Albert burst through the door. He clearly hadn't realized that James had found his way into the kitchen. As soon as he saw the blood covering the white tile floor, his eyes became panicked.

"I just came back to apologize for last night," James whispered in a monotone voice.

No matter how hard he tried, he couldn't draw his eyes away from the blood. I felt like an absolute monster. Never in my life, except maybe in the presence of that terrified girl on the night Nina had found me, had I ever been so sickened by the thought of what I was. James, sweet, innocent James, now knew that I was a vile, disgusting, nightmarish creature.

Albert's eyes darted to James. "Anne."

I knew precisely what he was thinking. Albert wasn't planning on letting James walk out of this room alive. James knew, and that made him a threat. But I couldn't let Albert do that. James was too good. He didn't deserve to die. None of this was his fault. James was just an innocent, well-meaning human.

I locked eyes with Albert from across the room. "No, Albert, no."

His eyes had turned dark. "We don't have a choice."

James was looking frantically between the two of us. "I won't tell, honestly. No one has to know. I won't tell anyone."

He was telling the truth. It was evident in his eyes. How was he so calm? If he'd been a normal person, he would have been screaming, running for the door. But for some reason, he was standing perfectly still.

Albert's voice had become menacing. "Why should we believe you?"

"Well, I'd rather not end up dead," James replied. "I mean, I totally didn't know any of this existed until five seconds ago, but I'm guessing that lying to a vampire probably isn't the best way to stay alive."

Why wasn't he panicking? It made me seriously worry about his self-preservation instinct. Maybe there was something wrong with his adrenal system.

I laughed sarcastically. "This is crazy." I turned to look over at Albert before continuing. "I'm actually going to go insane."

Albert crossed his arms over his chest. "You and

me both."

James looked skeptically between the two of us. "So, does this mean I'm not going to end up dead? Assuming I keep my mouth shut, which I definitely will."

For a moment, Albert looked determined to kill him. All of a sudden, his eyes softened. But an instant later, his emotionless glare was back.

"Fine," Albert grumbled.

James looked back over at me. "So since we've got that figured out, does that mean I can have a second chance? I promise I won't kiss you this time if you don't want me to."

He must have been crazy. There wasn't another explanation. Not five minutes ago, he'd found out I was a vampire. And for some bizarre reason, all he was concerned about was the fact that he'd kissed me.

"You kissed her?!" Albert roared.

This was going well. I had two men, both of whom I was attracted to, in one room. But the worst part was that one of them wanted to rip the other's throat out. That really was our most pressing concern. My complicated love life could wait until later.

"Albert, relax," I said.

For a moment, I hoped he would calm down. This didn't have to be a fight. The last thing I wanted was for them to hurt each other. I had no idea what was happening in my heart, but I knew I didn't want either of them to be in pain. The rest was too complicated to think about.

He shot me a look of pure disgust. "Don't you dare start with me right now, Anne."

I glared back at him. "I really don't think this is any of your business."

If he just stayed out of it, we could deescalate this situation. James had said too much, but he also hadn't done anything wrong. Albert was going too far. He didn't have any sort of claim on me. I was allowed to kiss whoever I wanted to.

He turned around and stormed toward me. "I'm not dealing with you at the moment." Albert pointed to James. "This boy has crossed a line."

Jealousy. That was it. This was pure, uncontrolled jealousy. He was only furious that James had touched me. It wouldn't have mattered if James was a human, wolf, or vampire; Albert despised him simply because his lips had touched mine.

I grabbed his arm. "What line is that, exactly?"

"Don't," Albert whispered.

My gaze locked with Albert's. His eyes pleaded with me to stop. He knew he'd made a mistake. Of all men, he had no supposed right to defend my virtue. I was no longer a teenage girl in 1950s Georgia. It wasn't the same. After all, we were both vampires.

"James, come on," I said, grabbing his hand and pulling him toward the door.

My heart ached as I walked away from Albert but

quickly recovered with the touch of James's gentle hand in mine. He didn't seem repulsed by the fact that he was touching a vampire. In fact, he seemed relieved.

"Don't do this, Anne. We both know how it ends," Albert shouted.

Maybe he was right, but what if he wasn't? Could I risk it? James was so special. I didn't want to give him up. I never had. I just didn't want to hurt him. In fact, I'd never wanted him to know the truth at all. But I couldn't go back and make him forget what had just happened. He knew my reality, and there was nothing I could do to change it.

As I opened the front door, I whispered, "No, no, we don't."

Chapter 6

FORTRESS

What do you do after the human boy who has a crush on you finds out you're a vampire? Well, I had absolutely no idea. The only thing I could think to do was take him back to my apartment. Nina and Anya were going to go absolutely crazy.

After we'd made it a little ways away from the cafe, I sent Katie a quick message telling her what had happened; she promised to have all of the blood cleaned up, so I didn't have to worry about it. After all, bloodstains spread over the kitchen floor weren't very good for business.

James walked silently beside me. He was probably speechless. That was a good thing because I wouldn't have known what to say to him. When he'd seen the blood, and everything had become all too obvious, he hadn't panicked or screamed. He'd simply accepted the fact that I was a vampire as if it were as trivial as saying I was allergic to peanuts. Honestly, I was probably more anxious than him about the whole situation.

James definitely had some sort of problem. Maybe the chemicals in his brain were off balance, or perhaps he had no self-preservation instinct at all. Either way, he needed some serious help. No rational human learned of the existence of vampires without panicking. It wasn't normal.

And what would I do about Albert? Prior to the disaster, I'd made up my mind that I couldn't be with James. He was human; it was just too dangerous. Besides, being with him would have meant that I would have to tell him what I was. But now that he'd discovered it on his own, things were different. Whatever had happened between Albert and me would have to be sorted out later.

Still, I couldn't get him off my mind. Albert was like a song stuck in the back of my head. No matter how hard I tried, I couldn't drown him out. He was always there, always present. I wanted to push his presence from my mind, but he was stuck to me like glue.

As we approached the apartment, James spoke, "So, where are we going?"

I opened the door to the building, letting him inside. "To my apartment. I share it with my sisters. Adopted sisters, actually."

"Vampires?" James asked.

I nodded. At this point, there was no reason to hide much of anything. "Yes."

As we stepped into the elevator, he reached for my

hand. Without giving it much thought, I let him take it. He gently rubbed his thumb across the back of my hand. How was he so calm? It was entirely incredible. Though I didn't respond, he kept his fingers linked through mine.

James was really starting to worry me. I wasn't sure whether his unnatural calmness was good or bad. There was something slightly scary about his reaction. If he had run away from me, I might have felt better.

His eyes met mine. "What are you going to tell them? Your sisters, I mean."

I was wondering about that, too. Would I just walk in and declare that I'd brought home a human? They probably wouldn't mind, but they'd be shocked. I didn't want to make a scene, but there wasn't much else to do.

"Oh, Nina and Anya, I won't need to tell them much of anything," I replied.

His eyes grew wide. "They're not going to think I'm like, um…the meal, are they?"

I suppressed a laugh; at least he was displaying a bit of self-preservation now. "No, we don't do that."

He bit his lip. "So, you don't like corner people and drain their blood?"

I squeezed his hand. "No, most of us don't. At least, uh, not like that."

He looked a bit confused but didn't ask me to elaborate. That was good; I really wasn't in the mood to explain the consensual-feeding situation. Way too much had already happened today.

A few moments later, the elevator door opened, and we stepped onto the third floor of my apartment building. As I unlocked the door to the apartment, I took one last, deep breath. The door swung open to reveal our bohemian-style home. Anya's hanging plants and tapestries decorated the yellow walls, while the scent of Nina's lemon candles filled the room. Lamps and lanterns lit the space; I'd always hated industrial lighting. The hardwood floors were almost entirely covered in a selection of rugs chosen by Nina. Anya had demanded that we have a fish tank. So underneath the TV in the living room sat her huge, aquamarine habitat. Our Ragdoll cat, Snuffles, was staring up at it, as usual.

Off to the left of the living room and kitchen were our three bedrooms. Nina and Anya actually had beds in theirs, but only for when Roy and Arthur spent the night. Nina's room was painted a gentle caramel color with a giant canopy bed, covered in pillows of all shapes and sizes, in the back. Oil paintings from India adorned the walls, along with bookshelves filled with classics. Along the exterior wall, she had a pretty window seat where she often sat to write. Her room always smelled of cinnamon, which was part of the reason I enjoyed being in there so much. The atmosphere was entirely calming.

Anya's room was right beside Nina's and painted a soft, cream color. In the center of the room was a circular hanging bed. Fairy lights were draped across the walls, which held floating bookshelves. We all enjoyed reading, though Nina and I preferred novels while Anya enjoyed books on philosophy, ethics, and history. In the corner of the room sat her collection of succulents. She was really very passionate about them. Her room was peaceful, too. It was simple, clean, and refreshing.

My room was across the hall from both of them. It was a light pink color, with built-in bookshelves lining the walls. A French-style vanity sat beside the large window. I also had a purple, Victorian chaise where I did the majority of my reading. To fill up the remainder of the empty space, I'd placed a pink velvet camelback sofa and a mahogany coffee table in the center of the room. The extra furniture helped to make up for the lack of a bed. My strange little room was one of the only places on earth where I felt truly safe to be myself. In the confines of those four walls, I could really breathe.

To the right of the living room and kitchen was our bathroom. It was white marble with a pink clawfoot bathtub and a pedestal sink. On the far side of the room was a large window covered by floor-length curtains. We'd all wanted a nice bathroom. After all, what did vampires have to do in the middle of the night other than take ridiculously long bubble baths? It's not like we were going to turn into bats and fly away. That was absurd.

Nina was sprawled on the couch, her laptop beside her. She operated an incredibly successful online jewelry store. Each of her pieces were custom made and simply beautiful. Her salary alone could have supported us, but

I had never been able to come to terms with staying home all day. I needed my little waitress job for my mental health if nothing else. Roy was asleep beside her. She was gently stroking his golden hair as he slept.

After laying my bag down on the counter, I led James over to Nina. She was entirely immersed in what she was doing. But after a few moments, she glanced up. Her brown eyes grew wide in shock as she noticed James. A few seconds later, she winked at me. I shook my head and pursed my lips in response. If only she knew how we had ended up in this situation.

"James, this is my sister, Nina," I said.

James smiled brightly at her, "It's nice to meet you." He glanced down at his clothes before continuing. "I wasn't really expecting to meet you today. I would have tried to look better if I'd known."

It felt as if my frozen heart gave a little thud. This boy was too perfect, almost too kind. Next to him, I felt like nothing. There was no way I was good enough for him. Why was he trying this?

"Aww, you look fine. We're pretty relaxed around here, anyway," she replied.

Roy opened his bright blue eyes and smiled lazily at us. "Hey, Anne." He sat up and glanced at James. "Who are you?"

James held his hand out for a handshake. "I'm James."

Nina looked between the two of us with a grin on

her face.

"Well, I have to say, this place isn't exactly what I expected from a bunch of vampires. I was thinking there'd be more black or some paintings with blood splattered on them. Sorry, that probably sounds awful." James glanced over at me with an apologetic expression on his face.

At least he was starting to sound rational. Not that we would have kept blood-splattered decor — we weren't barbarians. But he was right. He should have been afraid of us. Maybe not Nina and Anya, but definitely me. I wasn't safe.

Roy burst into laughter. "I like him already."

Nina raised her eyebrows. "You told him?"

I sighed. "Not exactly. He kind of found out on his own."

She grinned. "I should have guessed that. Knowing you, it could have taken ages before you told him yourself."

"Thanks for the huge vote of confidence," I mumbled.

James picked up Snuffles, holding the cuddly bunch of fur against him. He started purring, nuzzling his head against James's chest.

Moments later, the apartment door flew open, followed by Anya and Arthur bursting inside. Snuffles jumped from James's arms and onto the floor. Nina gave them a questioning glance. What else had gone wrong?

Whatever this catastrophe was, it was certainly fitting with the theme of the day.

Anya threw her purse into an armchair. "I absolutely detest her! She'd really done it this time!"

Nina raised her eyebrows. "Pansy?"

"Who else?" Anya replied.

"Who's Pansy?" James whispered in my ear.

"Um, well, Roy and Arthur are werewolves. Arthur's the alpha of the pack. Pansy and her brother, Dale, are both wolves who enjoy pushing Anya's buttons," I answered.

"What did she do now?" Nina asked, glancing down at her nails.

This was a rather normal occurrence. Pansy and Anya got along about as well as cats and dogs. In other words, they despised each other. There was always some sort of arguing between the two of them. I'd never actually met Pansy, but from what Nina and Anya had told me, she caused problems simply for the fun of it. She drove Arthur crazy, too.

"She convinced Dale to challenge me as alpha," Arthur replied.

I froze, not sure how to react. That was not what I'd been expecting. Why would she do that? Pansy knew just as well as everyone else what the stakes were.

The room fell into silence. Roy and Arthur were staring at each other, neither one of them saying a word. Anya was standing by the fish tank, fuming. Nina hadn't taken a single breath since Arthur had spoken. James, observing the climate of the room, hadn't moved a muscle.

"Why?" Nina asked hesitantly.

"Me," Anya said. "Because he's with me. She's stuck up and jealous that he wants me instead of one of the girls in the pack."

Vampires and werewolves. The drama was endless. Would we ever get over it? Probably not. But after years of living with this never-ending conflict, I was sick of it. Of course, most of us got along perfectly fine. It was only people like Pansy, who had a true superiority complex, that caused problems. Pansy thought that she and her friends were better than Anya. That was all there was to it.

Roy sighed. "It's been an issue for a while, but I never thought she'd actually do something about it."

James was watching the discussion with a sort of astonished excitement on his face. I had nothing to say. This was bad, very bad. Arthur could get really hurt if not killed. Packs were ordered and controlled by a strict hierarchy. The position of alpha was passed from father to son. It was almost monarchical. On occasion, the alpha would have his leadership challenged. It generally ended in a bloody, savage fight. Sometimes, one of the wolves would end up dead.

Everyone had known that Pansy was infuriated when Arthur and Anya had become official. Most vampires and wolves got along in relative harmony. Relationships between the two groups were common. But there were some on both sides of the aisle who were repulsed by the other. Pansy was one of the few wolves who really hated vampires.

"What are you going to do?" Nina asked.

"Obviously, I have to fight him," Arthur replied.

"You'll win," Roy said.

Arthur nodded. "I know, but people are going to get hurt."

We didn't need this in our lives. It was hard enough preventing our world from crumbling down. I had enough to deal with figuring what exactly I was going to do with James, no less Albert.

"Everything has to be complicated, doesn't it?" Nina moaned.

"When is it?" Roy asked.

"Tonight," Anya replied.

"We're going with you," Nina insisted.

James's eyes grew wide. "Does that include me?"

No, no, no, I thought. Why did he look excited? Yes, his voice held a bit of anxiety. But overall, he looked downright enthusiastic.

Arthur's face grew tight in confusion. "Who are you?"

"His name is James. Anne brought him home," Nina replied.

Arthur's eyes looked as if they might pop out of

his head. "Anne brought someone home?"

Was I seriously that much of a hermit? To be honest, I thought I was really branching out. I'd even started wearing skirts that showed my thighs.

I wanted to bang my head against the wall. "None of this is even kind of important right now."

Arthur shrugged. "I don't care. He can come."

My jaw dropped. How was this happening to me? This had to be some sort of bizarre nightmare. James didn't belong anywhere near this werewolf-gladiator battle. He was human, and I wanted to keep him that way. Preferably with his limbs attached, too.

"Cool, I'm in. Assuming no one's going to try to rip my throat out after they've turned into a giant dog, right?" James asked.

Roy grinned. "Don't worry, we got you."

How had this day gone so drastically wrong? First with the Albert situation, then the whole blood ordeal, and now with taking James into a werewolf fight. This was the exact opposite of what I'd intended. But at this point, I had no choice other than to let the cards fall where they may. I'd already tried my best to keep James far away from my world, but he'd found his way right back into it. All I could do now was keep him safe in the middle of the chaos.

He didn't belong here. He should have been hanging out with a human girl, going to parties, studying, or pretty much anything else that wasn't life-threatening.

Werewolf fights were not a leisurely activity. Actually, neither was wandering around with a bunch of vampires. It wasn't safe for him, but he didn't seem to care. James was determined to be a part of this, and it seemed there wasn't much I could do about it.

Chapter 7
THE CHALLENGE

"You look amazing," James whispered.

I couldn't help but smile as he looked at me with wonder in his eyes. If a little bit of effort was all it took to make his eyes light up, it was worth it. The way he looked at me with such sheer admiration was incredible. It made me feel alive.

I'd changed into a red mini-skirt, tights, black tank top, and tall velvet boots. My curls toppled down my back like a midnight waterfall. Nina stood beside me wearing white jeans, a pink leather tube top, and wedge heels. Her raven hair fell down to her shoulders like a silky curtain. Anya was looking into the mirror, adjusting her already flawless purple mini-dress. She'd pulled her hair up into space buns and topped them with golden butterfly hairpins. This was a show, and we had to dress the part.

Alpha challenges were a once-in-a-lifetime sort of event. Wolves from all of the surrounding packs would be in attendance. It was a little bothersome how excited people got to watch two men fight to the death, or at least until one conceded. But even so, it was about more than the fight itself. There were politics involved and so many people to impress. The better you presented yourself and your family, the more likely they were to support you. It never hurt to be intimidating.

I smiled at James. "Thanks."

He huddled close to me as Nina applied lipstick and Anya slipped on her stilettos. Of course, I didn't want James to go with us. I still wasn't exactly sure how my plan to isolate him for his safety had come crashing down in only a few hours. There was nothing I could do about it now. Until I could figure out what to do, I had to make sure he didn't get hurt. So for the moment, that meant keeping him by my side.

"Is this what you normally wear to a...um, werewolf fight club?" James asked.

Even after this long, crazy day, he was still beautiful. Not in a feminine sense, but just in measure of attractiveness. Yes, he was gorgeous. Long lashes erupted above his emerald eyes, bringing out the most remarkable feature in his tall, circular face. Each time he smiled, his lips formed into a small grin before he let out a low laugh. And when he brushed his blond hair to the side, I felt a warm feeling creep into my chest. Handsome didn't seem to fit him. No, he was beautiful.

I laughed. "I suppose."

"Everyone ready?" Anya asked.

Arthur nodded. "Let's go."

Before we left the apartment, James laced his fingers through mine. I thought about pulling away but couldn't bring myself to do it. I wanted to hold his hand. Maybe I was a little selfish, but I wanted him to comfort me. It seemed silly, the human reassuring the vampire. We had such an odd dynamic.

We arrived in an open field outside of the city. When we stepped out of our cars, there were already fifty or so people there. Many of the faces, friendly or not, were familiar. Most of the unfriendly spectators whispered as we walked by. Anya held Arthur's hand firmly in hers as we made our way into the center of the crowd. As far as I could tell, James was the only human in attendance. A few wolves looked at him skeptically. Before they had the chance to say anything, I let my fangs fall in front of my lips, hissing quietly. They looked repulsed, but I didn't care. My focus was on protecting James.

As the crowd began to back away, Pansy stepped forward. Her black jeans, green top, and high-heeled combat boots made her look more menacing than she actually was. In reality, her five-foot frame was fragile and small. Her pixie cut and pink cheeks didn't exactly increase her scariness either. Still, she tried her best to look intimidating.

Dale, with his gruff-looking beard and deep frown, stood beside her. The moonbeams shone down upon us as we prepared to witness the fight of our lives. Arthur and Dale examined each other, both waiting for the other to speak.

The tension was sharp. I could almost hear the anxiety floating through the air. A burst of lighting might have been appropriate. I wouldn't have been shocked if a thunderstorm appeared out of nowhere.

"Dale…," Arthur began.

He responded with a slight nod. There wasn't any reason to outline the specifics of the situation. Everyone, except James, knew how these fights worked. Without a moment's hesitation, Arthur pulled off his T-shirt and handed it to Anya. She threw it in the bag at her feet with the rest of his extra clothes. He'd need them after he changed back. Both of the boys stood facing each other, wearing nothing more than battered pairs of jeans. Pansy had an overconfident smirk on her face. I couldn't tell if it was real or not.

They both took a few steps back, leaving a decent space between them. Moments later, they took off running. Shouts, screams, and whistling could be heard throughout the crowd as their bodies transformed into wolves. James was staring at them in pure shock. Not knowing what else to do, I took his hand in mine.

They crashed to the ground, Arthur landing with his paw planted firmly on Dale's chest. He stood growling, their faces only inches apart. He was giving him another chance to back out. If this fight ended badly, none of it would be Arthur's fault. An instant later, they were rolling on the ground. Snarling could be heard above the shouts of the crowd.

Nina was standing with her arms around Anya. Anxiety was plastered on Anya's sweet heart-shaped face, while Nina looked ahead with determination in her mahogany eyes. I stood beside them, with James right behind me. He was as perfectly still as a human could be, and I was slightly worried that he might stop breathing altogether.

Screams and cheers could be heard throughout the crowd as they collided with each other again, again, and again. Every time Dale's jaws clenched around Arthur's wolf form, Anya winced. Roy had his eyes locked on the two of them. His muscles were tensed as if ready to jump into the fight at any second. But he couldn't have even if he wanted to. Alpha challenges went until someone conceded or died.

Drops of blood began to fall to the ground as they ruthlessly clawed each other. I bit my lip, trying my best to ignore the blood. Even in the midst of the chaos, it was the one thing my mind wanted to focus on. Nina and I shared a brief glance, both holding our breath. It would be better if we tried not to breathe—we didn't need the oxygen, anyway. Anya didn't even seem to notice its alluring scent. She was so intensely focused on Arthur that no amount of blood could have drawn her attention away from him.

As the fight raged on, it only got more brutal. Pansy was barking orders at her brother, screaming at him to end it. A few others joined her. Roy was surrounded by a group of male wolves cheering Arthur on. Both sides raised the energy so high that it could have powered light bulbs. Anxiety filled my chest.

Dale clawed at Arthur's eyes, causing Anya to scream. Nina pulled her tight into her arms. Pansy was standing with a few other girls laughing. Roy grimaced as his brother howled in pain.

In a flash too quick for human eyes to process, Arthur burst from underneath Roy and pinned him to the ground. There was blood dripping from his face as he growled. Dale struggled to free himself, but Arthur was too strong. His alpha growl sent shivers into the hearts of everyone present. Arthur was giving Dale every possible chance. He didn't want to kill him, but there was nothing he could do to make him concede.

Arthur rose up with a terrifying growl, ready to slash Dale's throat, when Pansy screamed, "Stop!"

She raced toward her brother, falling on the ground and wrapping her arms around him. Half a second later, his form receded into his human body. Pansy wrapped a blanket around him, tears streaming down her face, and she collapsed onto his chest. Arthur gave one final growl before turning away from them and walking toward the trees.

For several minutes, everyone stood in stunned

silence. As Arthur returned from the woods in his human form, wearing a pair of torn jeans, raindrops began to fall softly from the sky. There was blood on his face and cuts scattered all over his upper body. But still, he looked better than Dale. Anya ran toward him, throwing her arms around his neck as he pulled her against him.

Arthur held Anya's hand as he walked up to where Pansy was still collapsed on the ground with Dale. His eyes held fire.

"I hope that settles things," he said in his deep, overpowering voice.

Dale looked down at the ground. "Yes."

Arthur nodded before leading Anya through the crowd of werewolf onlookers and back toward us. Roy nodded at him with a small smile on his face. Nina clung to Roy's arm, smiling. James, who I'd almost forgotten was with us, finally seemed to relax. He's been practically frozen the whole time, but he was starting to loosen up. I still held his hand in mine. He looked down at me with a glint of hope in his soft green eyes.

Arthur turned to address the crowd. "Time to go home, everybody. There's nothing more to see here."

"I agree. It's definitely time to go home," Nina added. She leaned up to place a gentle kiss on Roy's cheek, "Are you staying over?"

He lifted Nina's chin to kiss her. "Yes."

Nina smiled as she took his hand and started pulling him toward the cars. Arthur and Anya followed behind them with his arm around her back. James and I hurriedly kept up with them, anxious to leave the depressing scene.

We arrived back at the apartment with everyone entirely exhausted. Arthur practically collapsed on Anya's bed. She followed behind him, laying his head on her lap as he fell into a deep sleep. Roy sat on the couch to watch TV but quickly drifted off. Nina cuddled close to him, wrapping a blanket around them both. James, who had hardly spoken since we'd left for the fight, was trying to appear as if he wasn't tired. But in reality, he looked awful.

"Come on, I'll drive you home," I said.

Though he seemed as if he wanted to protest, he knew he was too exhausted to argue. The fact that his eyelids were drooping was evidence that he needed sleep.

I slid into the driver's side of my Corolla as James clumsily collapsed into the passenger seat.

"Tired?" I asked.

He sighed. "Very."

I pulled out of the driveway before speaking again. "How do you feel about what you saw tonight?" My tone was somber. He had to understand the meaning of this conversation.

"To be honest, it was terrifying. But it was extraordinary, too. I've never seen anything as fascinating, except maybe you," James answered in an honest tone.

That same warm, heavy feeling descended upon my abdomen. It was like someone had lit a candle inside of me. I couldn't seem to control it.

My heart began to flutter, but I quickly shoved it back down. "Do you realize how dangerous it was for you to be there?"

His eyes scrunched in confusion. "It was dangerous for you, too."

I shook my head. "No, you don't understand. If I'd needed to, I could have fought my way out of there. In twenty seconds, I could have killed five of them. I was safe. You, on the other hand, were like a dove surrounded by lions. There are literally an endless number of ways you could have ended up dead."

He pursed his lips. "Then why did you bring me?"

I glanced at him. "What else was I supposed to do with you?"

He was silent for a few moments. "I don't need you to babysit me, Anne."

Neither of us knew what to say. I hardly wanted him to think that I saw him as weak; he wasn't. For a human boy, he looked strong and well-toned. He probably could have won a fistfight easily—with a human, that is. His body was twice the size of mine, and he towered over me. But even with all of that, he was still human. It hadn't anything to do with size or level of fitness. On the contrary, it was about his humanity.

"I don't want you to get hurt because of me," I

whispered.

"Pull over," he replied.

I pulled the car to the side of the road and turned toward him. "This isn't safe. I shouldn't even let myself be alone with you."

He took my hands in his. "Anne, you're what I want. Human or not, I think you're so, so beautiful. There's nothing you could do to convince me otherwise."

I wanted so badly to let myself fall into this. He talked about me as if I was the brightest star in his galaxy. It seemed like I was the only girl he saw, the only one he wanted.

I attempted to pull my hands away, but he wouldn't let me. "I'm too dangerous for you."

He shook his head. "I don't believe that."

What? Did he just not see it? I was literally a monster, yet he refused to admit it. Was it my small size, or just his denial? I had no idea what to say.

"You're not dangerous," he whispered.

It didn't matter if he refused to acknowledge it. The truth was still the same. Perhaps he still hadn't realized exactly how nightmarish I was.

I turned my head away from his. "You wouldn't know. I'm a monster, James. A monster."

"No, Anne. You're gorgeous," he replied. "And I'm going to prove it to you."

My eyes met his. "Oh no, you're not. You're going to get some common sense and run. You don't belong in this mess."

"What if I want to be in it?" he whispered.

I bit my lip, taking in a gulp of air for the first time in a while. He smelled so good. I pulled myself as far away from him as I could in the tiny space. The temptation was everywhere.

He noticed my change in posture. "How long has it been since you've eaten?"

My eyes grew wide. This was bad, very bad. I'd been so distracted that I'd forgotten to eat. How could I have been so stupid?

"You're hungry. It's okay," he whispered.

He unbuckled his seatbelt, moving closer to me. I shook my head, firmly closing my mouth. He had to be insane if he thought I would actually do it. Why did he want this? It was crazy.

"It's all right, Anne. I don't want you to starve," he said.

He tilted his head to the side, leaving his neck exposed. This was just absolute madness. He didn't know what he was doing.

"No, no, James," I whispered. "You don't know what you're asking for."

He smiled gently. "It's okay. I saw bite marks on Roy's neck. Nina bites him, and he seems fine."

I should have thought about that. If he hadn't seen them, this wouldn't have been an issue. Of course, now I couldn't exactly deny it.

"That's different," I replied.

His eyes locked with mine. "How?"

Wasn't it obvious? Arthur and Roy were wolves. Biting them wasn't an atrocity.

"You're human. And besides, we're not even together," I answered.

His breathing was heavy. "I want to be."

He moved even closer to me. My back was pressed against the car door, and all I could smell was him. His sweet, alluring scent was everywhere. I felt my fangs slide out of my mouth and slice my bottom lip. I had never wanted James to see this. He thought I was beautiful, but now he'd think I was disgusting.

"It's okay," he whispered.

He put his hands around my waist and pulled me toward him. I didn't have the self-control to resist. I barely realized what was happening. His hands wrapped around my back as my fangs sunk into his neck. Within moments, we became wrapped in euphoria.

The sweetness was completely overwhelming. It was better than anything I'd ever tasted. He whispered my name over and over again as he gently rubbed my back. There was no way I was going to be able to pull myself away from him. I just didn't have that much strength.

He ran his hands through my hair, sighing softly. It was just as good for him as it was for me. In that moment, I thought I had glimpsed a little sliver of Heaven. There didn't seem to be anything in the world that could have been better. His scent, smell, and taste were practically flawless.

"Anne," he whispered.

His voice had grown weak. Instantly, I came back to reality. I was taking too much from him. It took an unbelievable amount of effort, but I managed to pull myself away from his body. I threw myself as far away from him as I could, pressing my back against the car door. What had I done?

He slumped back in the seat, turning his head toward me. His emerald eyes were sparkling like stars on a clear summer night. Our eyes locked together as if they were tied by some sort of invisible string.

He smiled lazily at me. "We should do that more often."

Had he gone completely crazy? I could have killed him. It had been a horrible mistake. I clearly couldn't control myself.

I looked at him in shock. "Are you insane?! That never should have happened. I could have killed you!"

He looked at me gently. "But you didn't. I trust you, Anne."

I shook my head. "You shouldn't. I'm a monster, James. That can't happen again. I won't let myself do that to you. The last place you should be is anywhere close to me."

He looked like I'd slapped him. "I want to be close

to you. Shouldn't I be able to decide what I want to do with my life?"

My eyes met his. "Not when what you want has a high likelihood of killing you."

It was so hard to tell him no. I wanted him, wanted his blood. But at the same time, I wanted him to be safe. That was more important.

He glanced down at his hands. "It's that other guy, isn't it?"

I raised my eyebrows. "Albert? No, it's not that, James. This is about keeping you safe."

Looking down at my shirt, I could see a few drops of blood splattered on it. I bit my lip; it was entirely repulsive. James deserved better than this. I was bad for him. He thought I was what he wanted, but he was wrong. All he truly desired was to be loved. I wasn't the right person to give him that. He deserved a girl, a human girl, who could give him the type of life he deserved. A peaceful human existence was what he needed, whether he liked it or not.

"Anne, look at me," he whispered.

Our eyes met again, this time with such an intensity that it scared me. This was so, so dangerous. But he looked so determined. How could I possibly communicate the reality of the situation to him? He just didn't seem to understand how crazy the whole concept was.

"I want you," he said in a voice so gentle that it almost made my frozen heart melt.

All I wanted was to tell him how badly I wanted him, too. But if I did, I'd never be able to walk away. There had never been a moment in my immortal life that I'd had a stronger desire to be human again. Oh, how sweet our love could have been.

The taste of his blood was still in my mouth. I hadn't had human blood in so long that it was almost intoxicating, but I had to fight it. This wasn't a time when I could let my instincts run wild. I'd already taken too much from him.

"Kiss me," he whispered.

I shook my head. "James, I can't. You don't know how hard this is for me."

Ignoring my protest, James moved closer to me. I held my breath and firmly pursed my lips. But oh, how badly I wanted to kiss him. If only I was human, this would be so much simpler.

"You won't hurt me," he whispered.

I closed my eyes, my lips still firmly pressed together. I wasn't going to give into this. He had to know I was serious. It just wasn't safe.

Moments later, his lips were gently on mine. His kiss was as light as a feather. It was just a soft, loving caress. I was frozen still, not letting myself move a muscle. But even so, he continued. James knew I wanted his love.

He pulled away, looking only slightly disappointed. A small smile was still displayed on his face. He was gorgeous, truly mesmerizing. I wanted him to hold me, to tell me everything would be okay. But no, I couldn't let myself hurt him.

"I'm sorry," I whispered so lightly that I wasn't sure he could even hear it.

He smiled. "It's okay, maybe next time."

There were a million things I wanted to say. I just didn't know how. What was I supposed to do? There was no easy answer.

He opened the car door. "I can walk the rest of the way. Besides, I can tell you have a lot to think about."

He gave me a small smile before stepping out into the warm night air and closing the door behind him. I sat there, slumped in my seat. James Hamilton had truly left me speechless.

Chapter 8
So Finite

The restaurant's lighting was so low that I almost felt comfortable. It was a vampire establishment just outside the city. My full glass of rabbit's blood, topped with a piece of lime, sat in front of me. I'd barely touched it. A persistent feeling of nausea was making it almost impossible to even think about drinking. It had been less than forty-eight hours since I'd seen James, and I was still slightly high from his blood. Still, I needed to make sure I was fed before he arrived. I couldn't let something like that happen again.

I glanced up as James entered the room. He would never be able to surprise me. I could smell him all the way across the room. The most expensive perfume in the world wouldn't have even come close to him.

He smiled at me before sitting down in the chair on the other side of the tiny, two person table. His beautiful eyes were glimmering in the candlelight, and his white-blond hair was combed back neatly. The baby-blue dress shirt he wore was almost exactly the same color as my empire dress. We looked like a matching pair.

"I missed you," he said in a tone filled with innocence.

This was going to be miserable. I wanted to run my fingers through his soft blond hair and let him hold me. But no, he needed to hear what I had to say. It was as if I was running a cheese grater across my heart.

"We need to discuss this," I said in as neutral a tone as I could manage.

He nodded. "I agree, but I don't think there's much to say. I love you."

My eyes grew wide. That had not been what I was expecting. Was he trying to make this as difficult as he could? I wanted him to love me so badly, but I couldn't let him. I had a nagging thought in the back of my mind that kept asking me if all this effort was worth it. But every time it floated to the surface, I tried to shove it back down.

"No, don't say that," I whispered. "You can't let yourself think that."

He shrugged. "It's not a matter of thinking. It's just the truth. I know it seems too early, but it's how I feel. You're unlike anyone I've ever known."

I knew that feeling. Loving someone wasn't always voluntary. It could throw your life into absolute chaos. There's no logic to it.

I shook my head. "No, James, no. Don't you see?

I'm not like you. It's not that we're different. If that was the only thing separating us, it would be all right. It's that I'm less than you. You're human. Humans cause destruction, but they also create beauty. Your mind is so finite yet so brilliant. You're able to love with such a beautiful passion. In some small way, I can feel what you feel. But with humans, emotions completely engulf them. Maybe it's wrong to feel so much, or maybe it's just a path to self-destruction. Either way, it's something I greatly admire. You possess a freedom I'll never have again. To take that away from you would be so terribly cruel."

His soft green eyes bored into mine. "You're wrong. I don't care what you say about good or evil. None of that matters. I want your heart, even if it doesn't beat. That's all I care about, Anne. The only thing I want in this life is to be able to love you. The least you can do is let me."

He looked so hopeful, so determined, and so in love. How was I supposed to do this? I felt like I was looking at an angel; he was so pure. This man deserved so much.

He took my hands in his. "Every time I close my eyes, all I see is you. Those sweet blue eyes of yours haunt me, Anne. I can't escape them any more than I can escape my need for oxygen. If I had nothing except you, it would be enough. You don't have to love me, that's okay. I just want to love you. If I live to be a hundred, I'll still love you. There's no one who could truly replace you."

No one had ever said anything like that to me. It was as if he knew exactly what I wanted to hear. I felt like a string went directly from my heart to his. We were being pulled together by something stronger than desire. It was almost innate. Everything about it felt right and wrong at the same time. I didn't even know how that was possible. It just seemed like something I had to accept. Every time he touched me, my body melted. He made me feel less frozen. With him, I felt like my heart had started to beat again.

"I don't know what to do," I whispered.

He stroked my cheek. "I do."

My body tensed as he leaned toward me. How was I letting this happen? I'd come here to tell him this was too dangerous, that I couldn't see him anymore. And somehow, he'd already made my courage disappear. Every time he smiled, I wanted to fall into his arms. His gentle lips were so tempting, and his hands were so tender as they held mine. James treated me like glass, even though I could have broken his bones with little effort. When our eyes met, I felt beautiful.

His lips touched mine, but this time he didn't stop. I let my lips part and kissed him back. It was the taste of everything beautiful and good. Like drinking from a well of pure, tropical water. How could I possibly say no to him?

"I love you," he mumbled with his lips against

mine.

James was only the second man to tell me he loved me. It had been so long since I'd heard those words. Everything within me lit up as if the sun had started to shine.

"It isn't safe," I whispered.

He stroked my hair. "Doesn't matter."

What was I supposed to say to that? He knew what I was, but he didn't care. The same day he discovered I was a vampire, he'd kissed me. It really seemed as if it didn't matter to him. He'd accepted my identity as if it was nothing more than an odd diet. It was entirely bizarre, but it was reality. He didn't think I was evil, terrifying, or menacing. When he looked at me, he saw a girl. And when I looked at him, I saw a boy.

He pulled away from me, relaxing back into his chair. A small grin was displayed on his face. I shook my head, laughing. Never in my life had I met a human like him. There had been no screaming, terror, or anger. A little bit of healthy fear, but he'd moved past that. Now, he acted like I was human. I felt seventeen again. It was phenomenal.

His thumb gently massaged the back of my hand. "I really do love you."

I smiled softly at him as I gazed into his starlit eyes. "I think I love you, too."

Chapter 9

CHANGE HIM

My hair was wrapped in a messy bun on the top of my head. After we'd left the restaurant, I'd changed into a pink sweatshirt and pajama pants with little pandas on them. Of course, I couldn't go to sleep, but I could relax. I had planned for a long, relaxing night reading Jane Eyre and listening to Marilyn Monroe.

Just as I was about to sit down with my book, someone knocked on the door. It was probably just Roy. He always seemed to forget his keys. Arthur was already asleep in Anya's room, so there wasn't really anyone else it could be.

Nina jumped up off the couch. "I'll get it."

As I sat down, Snuffles crawled onto my lap. I gently stroked his silky fur. He purred as I ran my hands across his smooth back.

The door clicked open. "Hey Nina, is your sister home?"

It was Albert. Nina stopped in stunned silence

before glancing back at me. I pursed my lips, put Snuffles on the floor, and walked over to the door.

Albert smiled at me as I came to stand beside Nina. He looked pristine in his gray suit. As always, his hair was a mess of brown curls. I glanced up into his dark eyes with a slight frown on my face.

"Well, I'll just leave the two of you alone then," Nina said, giving me a confused glance.

"Thanks," I mumbled.

Albert leaned against the doorframe, smirking.

"What's so funny?" I asked before stepping into the hallway and closing the door behind me.

He grinned even wider. "You're wearing panda pajama pants."

I rolled my eyes. "What do you want?"

He mockingly placed a hand over his heart. "So much rudeness from a southern girl, I'm shocked. Where's that Georgia peach hospitality? You Americans have always puzzled me."

I raised my eyebrows and crossed my arms. If I listened closely enough, I could still hear the remnants of his age-old British accent. He chuckled, running a hand through his hair. Ever so slightly, I bit my lip. The memory of kissing him was slowly bubbling back up inside of me.

The joking manner left his face, leaving nothing but his dark, intimidating eyes for me to look at. I straightened my back, tilting my head to look up at him.

"I wanted to check on you after what happened with the human," he said.

The human? Was Albert just trying to infuriate me? James wasn't defined by his mortality. He had a name and an identity.

I pursed my lips. "His name is James."

Albert's face grew hard. "Defending him now, are we?"

Albert was leaning over me, his arms blocking me against the wall. He was so much taller than me that his chest was planted right in front of my face. I tilted my head up as high as I could to look into his dark eyes. A chill ran across my pale skin.

I could feel the anger rising in my chest. "Someone has to."

"He's just a boy, Anne," Albert whispered.

I rolled my eyes. "Oh please, you're the last person I want criticism from. Everyone knows you've been with more girls than you can remember. You're what, a hundred and eighty now? I've seen you with plenty of seventeen-year-old wolves. You have no right to judge."

Albert crossed his arms. "He's human. You know it's different."

It was different. Albert was right. But even so, I seemed to be incapable of keeping James separated from the supernatural world.

I looked into his intimidating eyes. "He's happy."

Albert raised his eyebrows. "So, you're going to

change him."

Fury coursed through me. "Absolutely not."

No, I couldn't do that to James. He could still change his mind at any instant and run the other way. I had no right to take that opportunity away from him. To watch his heart stop would be agonizing. The pain would be unbearable. He deserved so much better than to be transformed into a creature of stone. The sound of his heartbeat was too beautiful.

Albert threw his hands up in the air. "Then what are you doing? He'll either end up dead or changed. If you want to be with him, those are your two options."

"He'll be perfectly fine," I hissed.

Albert shook his head. "I can't believe you're doing this. It's so totally irrational. Not like you at all, Anne."

I scoffed. "Again, you have no room to talk."

Albert froze. "Is it because he can't bite you?"

I took a step back. "Don't be crazy."

Anger flooded his face. "I was so, so close. If he hadn't gotten in the way, everything would be different." He turned toward me with frustration in his eyes. "You only want him because he can't scare you the way I did."

I shook my head. "That's not true."

A look of realization crossed his face. "You're biting him, aren't you?"

I bit my lip, glancing at the floor. This conversation was going badly in so many different ways.

He leaned closer to me so that our faces were only

inches apart. "You are, aren't you? You're drinking from him."

I looked up at him. "It was only once, and—"

"Stop," he interjected. "I don't care."

He put his arms on either side of me, cornering me against the door. His eyes were stormy, and his face held clear frustration. I should have been afraid of him, but I wasn't. His cool body was so close to mine that I could practically feel its chill against my own icy form.

"You're such a hypocrite, Anne," he growled.

I shook my head, but before I had a chance to respond, he kissed me. Again, I noticed how different it was from kissing a human. Albert was certainly an expert. But this time, he wasn't treating me softly. It was blissful and infuriating at the same time. Part of me wanted him, and another was determined to be with James.

Only a moment later, I pushed him away. "Stop!"

Determination shone through his deep, dark eyes. "I know you want me. You've proved it."

He dropped his hands and took a step back. His lips were tight with anger. In some small way, he did scare me. Maybe it was because part of what he was saying was true. Either way, I didn't have time to worry about it.

"Albert, just stop," I whispered.

"Stop what?" Albert growled. "Stop making you realize the truth? Stop telling you what a stupid decision you're making?"

Frustration was rising inside me. He was pushing too hard. I didn't want to hear what he had to say. He had absolutely no right to criticize my choices after all the disastrous relationships he'd had.

"You don't know what I need! I can't come to terms with you being you!" I screamed.

"You have no idea," he hissed. "Because after all this time, you still haven't realized I'm in love with you."

My jaw dropped. We simply stood there staring at each other. I honestly had no idea what to say. He was in love with me? No, that couldn't be. He was just infatuated. He thought I was pretty. That was all. Everyone knew he liked to flirt.

Albert gently took my face in his hands. "I do truly, honestly, love you."

There was nothing I could say. I was so stunned that all I could do was stare at him. My hands shook as he moved closer to me. He placed a soft kiss on the top of my head before stepping away.

He looked at me pleadingly. "Please, Anne, please. I want you, I love you, and I'm better for you than him."

I still had no idea what to say. For several moments we stood in silence. His eyes were a mixture of anger, terror, and hope. I didn't want to tell him, no, but I had to. I loved James, and I couldn't deny that. Even though it disappointed Albert and hurt me to do so, there was no way I could change the reality of the situation.

He leaned back against the wall. "That night in the

club, I really thought you were going to be mine." He sighed, looking down into his hands. "The first time we kissed, I was sure of it. But now, I know it meant nothing to you."

"That's not true," I whispered.

It meant so much. Passion had been released within me, blowing my world into a swirl of love, terror, and excitement. Each kiss he'd given me had whispered the secrets of my heart.

Albert glanced over at me. "I don't have the energy to deal with you right now."

He turned around, walking toward the elevator. His hands were balled into fists as he walked. Everything about his posture communicated anger. Yet I wanted to go after him. I didn't want him to be in pain because of me. Why was this all so complicated?

"Where are you going?" I yelled.

"The club," he replied without glancing back over his shoulder.

A few seconds later, the elevator door shut behind him.

With my back against the apartment door, I slid down to the floor. Holding my head in my hands, I attempted to come to terms with my newly overwhelming love life.

Chapter 10

PRECIOUS HEARTBEAT

I laughed as James pulled me out of the movie theater and back into the night. That had been the worst romantic comedy I'd ever seen, but it hardly mattered; I'd been with James. That was the only reason I'd gone.

Within the last three weeks, we had watched many movies, been to a concert, spent lots of nights together on the sand, and smiled more than I imagined possible. It was phenomenal. In only twenty-one days, we had grown to adore each other beyond what I could explain. Our trust had developed, too.

He held my hand as he smiled and pulled me into an alley. Slowly, his arms wrapped around my back. I giggled as he kissed my cheek, pulling me closer.

"Come on, Anne," he whispered into my ear.

I placed a soft kiss on his lips. "What?"

They were soft, pink, and sweet. Every time we kissed, his lips held the flavor of sugar. It was overwhelming, mind-blowing, and miraculous. I loved him so much.

"Bite," he whispered.

I pursed my lips. "James...."

He grinned. "Aww, come on."

His lips met mine again as he ran his hands through my black curls. I wrapped my fingers around his silky blond hair, kissing him back. His lips tasted like honey on a warm summer night. It was entirely blissful.

"Please," he whispered.

I sighed. "Well, maybe just one little bite."

James smiled brightly at me before tilting his neck to the side. We both wanted it so badly. Biting him was one of the most overwhelmingly spectacular sensations I'd ever experienced.

My fangs sunk into his neck, causing him to gasp in pain. But within a few moments, the pain was replaced with peacefulness. I'd never be able to describe to him just how euphoric it felt to have his arms wrapped around me as I tasted his sweet, precious blood. He couldn't possibly fathom how wonderful it was.

His fingers were tangled in my hair while my hands were tingling from the innumerable number of sensations flowing through me. I'd never felt so close to anyone in my whole life.

"Anne." He breathed my name as if it were the most glorious thing he'd ever heard.

I didn't have to try very hard to imagine the bliss enclosing around his mind. James was probably entirely immersed in the pleasure of it all. I suddenly realized just why Nina and Roy and Anya and Arthur enjoyed it so much. The bliss was absolutely incredible for both of us. I felt as if I were falling into a pool of rose petals, while he felt as if he were flying. What could have possibly been better?

My senses were immersed in his perfect, fantastical scent. Each time I inhaled, I was overwhelmed with the beauty of it all. He nuzzled his head against me as he sighed in total relaxation. Until this moment, I'd never realized just how much I wanted him. He was the one I was meant to spend forever with. I never wanted to stop loving him. This was how I wanted to spend the rest of my existence. James had become my everything, and I never wanted that to change. We were completely and wholly intoxicated with each other.

"Mind sharing?" a sultry female voice asked.

A vampire with long, braided brown hair and caramel eyes stood in front of me. Her fangs flickered out of her mouth as she grinned.

"Looks like there's plenty to go around," she whispered.

I threw James behind me, my fangs dripping with blood as I hissed at her. He froze, staring at her in shock. Our eyes locked as she began to back away.

She rolled her eyes, turning to glance down to the end of the alley. "Fine, I'll just get my own."

Before I had a chance to react, she approached a

man who had just walked out the back door of a bar. He grinned at her, glancing at her tight dress. His eyes grew wide as he took a sip of his beer. The man wasn't particularly attractive, but she didn't seem to care.

His words were entirely slurred. "Hey, gorgeous. Can I do something for you?"

She giggled. "Oh, just wait."

Moments later, she sank her fangs into his neck.

James was too shocked to scream. I wanted to pull him away so badly. He didn't need to see this. But I couldn't move. I had only just realized where I was. Yet again, I found myself in a dark, deserted alley. But this time, I wasn't the one dying.

The man didn't cry out or scream as the life was drained from his body. In fact, he looked relaxed. Then, I started to feel extremely sick.

Within just a few minutes, he was dead. She dropped his corpse on the concrete before licking the blood off her lips. As she started to walk back toward us, I pushed James against the wall, shielding him.

She laughed. "Better finish your meal before he runs away."

Moments after she disappeared into the night, I grabbed James's hand and began pulling him toward the car. He didn't protest but followed quickly after me. Neither of us were going to speak, not until we were safe. As soon as I'd gotten us both into the car, I quickly locked the doors and windows.

Up until tonight, I'd been sure that there was nothing in the world more dangerous to James than me. I'd thought that if I was capable of controlling myself, there was nothing that could hurt him. But that just wasn't true. I was bringing James, a human, into the supernatural world. There were any number of things that could happen to him.

"Anne," he whispered, "are you okay?"

I took a deep breath; the last thing I wanted to do was panic in front of him. He didn't even seem worried. His main concern was me.

"Don't worry about me. Are you all right?"

He nodded. "A little freaked out, but yeah. Honestly, that vampire girl was terrifying. Still, I was more worried about you. I didn't want her to hurt you to get to me."

Was there anything I could do to knock even a small bit of common sense into the man I loved? The last thing he should have been concerned about was me. I could have held my own. He, on the other hand, would have been as defenseless as a butterfly.

"I'd gladly die for you," I replied.

He looked at me in horror. "I'd never want you to."

I laughed sardonically. "That doesn't matter very much."

Our eyes locked together. His face held nothing but gentleness and love. Oh, how much I loved him. He was so good. I'd never be able to tell him how beautiful his soul was. Of all the people I'd ever met, he was one of the most pure of heart.

"You should let me protect you for a change," he stated flatly.

I rolled my eyes. "Okay, Captain America."

He ran his thumb across my cheek. "Anne, I'm not made of glass."

I looked up at him. "You wouldn't understand."

He pulled me toward him. "Help me to understand."

"If I hug you too hard, I'll break your ribs. If I kiss you too quickly, I'll cut your lips. And if another vampire gets to you when I'm not there to save you, you'll die," I whispered.

He shrugged. "So change me."

My jaw dropped. "No."

He looked at me in confusion. "Why not?"

I shook my head. "I refuse to take your life away."

"Anne, you wouldn't be. The life I want is by your side. There's no point to any of it if I'm not with you. So really, you'd be giving me the chance to live," he replied softly.

I could feel the tears begin to trickle down my face. "I will not be the one to make your heart stop."

He held my face in his hands. "You're what makes my heart beat."

The same tight, warm sensation was spreading

through my limbs up to my abdomen and then my chest. Heat rushed through me as I stared into his emerald eyes. They were so, so incredible. He was the most precious thing I'd ever held. This love was strong enough to hold us together, even though the world seemed to be trying to tear us apart.

James brought his lips to mine, kissing me with a gentleness I doubted lambs were capable of. It was so human. If I changed him, I'd be destroying something beautiful.

"Don't make me do this," I whispered.

He smiled lovingly as he stroked my hair. "Okay, we'll talk about it later."

As he softly kissed my cheek, I rested against his shoulder. With his warm arms tightly wrapped around me, I found myself desperately wishing that vampires could sleep.

Chapter 11
SPLIT IN TWO

The rising sun was one of the things I most enjoyed in my immortal life. Every morning while the world was still asleep, I'd stand on our little balcony to watch it make its ascent. Its rays gave warmth to my ice-cold skin. As the sun rose, it seemed to sing a song of life. The beauty of its light provided nourishment to the earth.

This was the first morning in a very long time when I'd been too preoccupied to greet the sun. James was asleep on the couch with his head on my lap. I gently stroked his hair as he slept blissfully. His pink lips were slightly parted, and I could see his eyelashes flicker as he dreamt. He looked as peaceful as a baby.

I knew what I had to say, but I was trying to ignore it. Even as I attempted to push it from my mind, the sense of anxiety wouldn't leave my chest. Albert's face kept resurfacing before my eyes. That conversation we'd had in the hallway kept haunting me. No matter how hard I tried, I couldn't forget Albert's words. And after what James and I had witnessed last night in the alley, I doubted this feeling of anxious nausea would be leaving me anytime soon.

I could sense James's breathing changing as he woke. He sighed softly before opening his eyes.

"Morning," he whispered with a glimmer in his green eyes.

I smiled gently. "Good morning."

His head still rested on my thighs. I ran my fingers through his perfect hair. As I traced the outline of his face with my eyes, he reached his hand up to touch my cheek.

"I love you," he said with a sleepy smile on his face.

I gave him a sad smile. "I love you, too."

He sat up, positioning himself beside me. "What's wrong?"

I glanced at his concern-filled eyes. "I'm worried about you, for you."

He looked confused. "Is this about what happened last night?"

I bit my lip. "Kind of."

He ran his thumb across my cheek. "Don't worry about that. It's okay."

I took his hand and pulled it away from my face. He looked a little wounded. "It's not okay."

He shook his head. "Anne—"

"No," I whispered, "you have to listen to me."

For the first time, I heard frustration in his voice.

"We already did this."

I pursed my lips. "Stop, James. Just listen."

He became silent, waiting for me to speak.

I nodded. "Thank you. What happened last night? That's what immortality looks like. We watched that man die as she literally sucked the life out of him. I've seen so, so many die that way, James. And not only that, but I've killed some of them."

For a brief moment, shock crossed his face. Only a few moments later, he regained his composure. It seemed as if there was nothing I could do to make him see the raw reality of what he was choosing.

I sighed. "Before Nina found me, I couldn't control my appetite. I somewhat limited myself to the less respectable members of society, but that's not an excuse. I completely lost any semblance of humanity. Now, maybe I have some of it back. But even so, it doesn't change the past. I've killed and watched many more die at the hands of others like me. That's what living forever gives you. You go through life if that's what you can call it, watching everyone around you die while you're frozen in this unbreakable, ice-like form. I don't want that for you. When you asked me to change you, I realized just how confused you are. Immortality isn't glamorous. It's death, so much death."

He shook his head. "Doesn't change anything. There's nothing you could say to make me stop loving you, so don't even try."

I looked into his eyes, preparing myself to say the words I so desperately wanted to bottle up inside. "I want you to choose someone else."

He looked taken aback. "There's no one else I want."

I anxiously ran a hand through my hair. "I'm sure there's lots of nice human girls. Girls that won't bring you into a world filled with death and darkness."

I felt sick as I looked away from him. This wasn't a conversation I wanted to have. The last thing I wanted was for him to leave. But that was selfish; he deserved to know that he had other options. And if I didn't highlight his ability to leave, I'd never be able to forgive myself.

He took my hands in his. "You're filled with light, Anne. You've made mistakes, just like everybody else. But you were able to make the most of a life you clearly didn't want. That's the difference between us. You never wanted this, but I do. I want you to change me; I want to be yours forever. If I can love you this much now, imagine how much I can love you when we truly have eternity in front of us."

I pulled away from him. "You're literally asking me to kill you. I won't do it. You're human. You have so many possibilities before you. Think about all that you could do. You could have a family, children, a life full of real, pure love. That's so much more than I can give you."

He wrapped his arms around my waist, pulling

me against him. "I want exactly what you can give."

I took a deep breath. "You're trying to give up your mortal life so you can spend eternity being dead."

He grinned. "Well, when you put it that way, it does sound a little strange."

I looked sternly at him. "This is not funny."

He pulled my body against his, kissing me stronger than he ever had before. I felt myself grow tense from shock. Eventually, I relaxed into it. He pulled me onto his lap, laying my legs on either side of him. His arms were wrapped firmly around my back, bringing me in closer. I'd never seen James like this before. He was strong, determined, and a little frustrated.

"This conversation is ridiculous," he whispered.

My forehead was pressed against his. "Only because you're being unreasonable."

He groaned. "Right."

I was about to pull away when he tangled his hands in my hair and urged me back. His lips pressed into mine in desperation and love. Heat flowed between us, letting our bodies melt and cling to each other. My mind was clouded by love. I truly felt as if I could just exist and let him hold me.

"What are you doing?" I whispered.

He kissed me again. "Proving that I'm not too weak for you."

My hands were wrapped around his neck. "I never said that."

James placed his hand between my shoulder blades and pulled me as close as possible. "You were thinking it."

I pressed my lips to his, leaning up against him. His taste was warm and compelling. James relaxed back against the couch, holding me to him. I loved him so, so much. Falling into a bed of flowers wouldn't have been as sweet as his touch.

"We're going to be okay," James whispered. "Do you trust me?"

"Yes," I mumbled.

"Here," he whispered, pulling his shirt to the side.

This conversation had not gone the way I had intended, but I was glad. We were going in circles, but one day it would stop. None of my urges for him to go were successful. That was all right, though. I'd never wanted him to leave. I'd only felt the obligation to encourage him. The words I'd spoken had not reflected the desires of my heart. Saliva was building up in my mouth. I couldn't resist, especially not when he was offering.

My teeth sunk into his neck, latching onto him. He gasped, his head falling back against the cushions. We both gave in to it, allowing ourselves to stop fighting against what seemed to be our inevitable future.

Again, the sweetness overwhelmed my senses. James was possibly the best thing that had ever happened to me. When his arms were around my body as I fed, I was sure he was the one meant to hold my heart.

He was my love, my angel, my soul split in two. Perhaps this was what true love felt like. If it was, I'd never be able to give it up. Maybe it was worth fighting an uphill battle for.

I pulled away from him, resting my head on his chest. "What do you want?"

He smiled lazily and laughed. "To go back to sleep."

I grinned. "I think I'm going to have to get a bed."

Chapter 12
Now

The sun was just starting to set as I untied my apron and laid it to the side. I shook my hair free from its braid, letting my curls fall gently around my face. After I unzipped my dress, I threw it over my sofa, grabbing a pair of yoga pants and an oversized T-shirt.

As I pulled my curtains to the side, revealing the pinkish-orange sky, Nina and Anya walked into the room. Anya plopped down on my chaise while Nina leaned up against the wall.

Anya wore a pair of silk pajamas, while Nina was dressed in a pink, cotton nightgown. They both had their hair falling freely down, making them look like two teenage girls ready for a sleepover. I grinned at the thought, remembering that they were both practically ancient.

"So...," Anya began with a hint of mischief in her voice.

Nina grinned. "How's it going with James?"

I raised my eyebrows, glancing between the two of them. "Good."

Anya giggled. "I totally didn't notice the bite marks on his neck."

I rolled my eyes playfully. "Oh please, Arthur's neck is practically decorated with them." I grinned at Nina. "Roy's too."

Anya's eyes glimmered. "Well, it is fun."

Nina smiled. "You two are getting serious."

"Mhm," I replied.

"So we were wondering," Anya began, "when are you planning to change him? I don't blame you if you want to wait a bit. The bite won't be half as good once he's changed. Might as well enjoy it while you can."

I crossed my arms. "Why does everyone keep asking that?"

It must have been the question of the week. For some reason, everyone seemed exceedingly interested in this topic. I just wanted to ignore it, but no one was willing to let me. It wasn't a particularly pressing issue, yet they all seemed to think it was.

Nina looked at me in confusion. "Well, if you want to stay with him, you'll have to do it."

I pursed my lips. "Why?"

They glanced at each other before Nina spoke. "He's going to die either way. Eventually, that is."

"Morbid," Anya muttered.

I shook my head. "But I don't have to be the one to

end his life."

There was a large difference between watching someone die and killing them. One implied guilt. The other didn't. Either would be painful, but killing him myself would require initiative. I didn't want to think about him dying. Of course, all mortals passed away. That was natural. But stopping his heart early just so I could change him into a creature of stone wasn't a part of the cycle of life.

Nina raised her eyebrows. "What does James think about it?"

I sighed. "He wants me to change him."

Anya rolled her eyes. "Come on, Anne. If he wants it, there's not much more to think about."

Why was this so simple to them? Even if he did want me to change him now, and I decided to let him make that decision, he might end up regretting it. If he didn't like immortality, he might resent me. I would have to live knowing that I had made his life miserable.

"I don't want him to end up hating me," I whispered.

Nina came over and wrapped her arms around me. "Anne, he won't. He loves you."

Anya licked her lips. "I think I'll give in to Arthur soon. He's been begging for it." She smirked. "That'll really tick Pansy off."

"Besides," Nina added, "James is seventeen. That's the same age you were."

"I didn't want it the way you did," I replied in a tone colder than I had intended.

Nina had voluntarily chosen her immortal life. As a young woman in eighteenth-century India, her parents had forced her to accept an arranged marriage. But the night before the wedding, she ran away. Lost and alone, she had stumbled upon the home of a beautiful spinster. After hearing Nina's story, the woman, a vampire, offered her immortality. In shock and awe, Nina had accepted her offer. I had heard the story a thousand times. It had never ceased to amaze me how both of my sisters had been given the choice to accept this life. If I had been given the same opportunity, I would have made a very different decision.

Anya had a similar transformation story, though it was a bit different. As a young Cherokee girl, Anya had fallen in love with a vampire. According to her story, he'd been old enough to remember ancient Rome. She had pleaded with him to change her so they could truly be together, and he had agreed. They spent decades together. But eventually, he abandoned her for another woman. Somehow, it hadn't dulled her enthusiasm for love.

Many times I wished I'd had the same choice as them. Because if I had been given the option, I would have kept my human life. But that hadn't been the way my story had gone.

"But he has a choice," Nina replied, "and this is

what he wants. I don't want to watch you give up the man you love because you're afraid. What happened to you, it was awful. But that's not what you'd be doing to James."

I could picture it. What if he woke up hating himself? He'd hate me, too. I couldn't take that. To know that I'd made him miserable, that I'd taken his life in vain, would be more painful than I could imagine. He would resent me for eternity. And after all that struggle, I'd lose him.

But I could see another future, too. A future where I would spend forever in the arms of my love. A reality that would make this immortal life no longer so hard to endure. I would have centuries to be loved by him. And maybe one day, I would forget how hard all of it had been. To know that we would never run out of time, that would bring a certain peace to my heart that I truly craved. I wanted James, and I wanted him forever.

"Anne," Anya whispered as she stroked my hair, "we love you. Nina and I want you to be happy. And if James is what makes you feel alive again, we don't want you to lose him."

What if I was overthinking this? Maybe they were right. I could make both of us happy for eternity with only a tiny drop of venom. He wanted to be changed so badly, and I wanted to be able to never stop loving him. We could make something beautiful. My family would finally feel complete.

Nina smiled. "Roy and I have been talking, and we've made a decision. I'm going to change him this month." She glanced over at Anya before turning back to me. "And, uh, we haven't told anyone yet, but we're getting married. We want to start our forever."

I could feel the grin on my face growing wider. "Nina, that's incredible. I'm so happy for you!"

Anya squealed. "Yes! We get to plan a wedding!"

I laughed. "I don't even know what to say."

Nina smiled softly. "Well, just think about what I told you. Remember, we want you to be happy."

I nodded. "Thank you, I will."

Anya grabbed Nina's hand and began pulling her out of my room. "Come on, we have to leave Anne to her melancholy contemplation. It's her favorite activity. Except for biting James, apparently. Besides, we have a wedding to plan."

Anya shot me a playful look before disappearing through the door. Nina smiled at me before following after her, shutting the door behind them.

I glanced out the window, admiring the rising moon. I'd always loved the stars. It made some sense; after all, we were children of the night.

So many choices and they all had to be made by me. If I changed him, I was taking a gamble. He would either end up hating me or loving me forever. There probably wouldn't be any in between. Was I willing to take that chance? Was he? Could I live with myself if he ended up regretting it? If I left him human, it was just a waiting game. He'd die eventually and be gone forever. Then, I'd never be able to get him back. There wasn't an easy choice. No matter what I did, it could end catastrophically.

I didn't really want him to be what I was. I could barely imagine living in a world where his heart didn't beat. But no matter which choice I made, it would end up being my reality. I could either turn him into a creature frozen in time or let him fade away. Either way, he would cease to be alive. I couldn't keep him here as a human forever. That just wasn't an option. If it was, my decision would have been simple.

Nina was going to change Roy. Neither of them had any problem with spending the rest of their existence as frozen statues. It didn't seem to bother them in the least. In fact, Roy seemed downright enthusiastic. He'd been asking Nina for years. They had been waiting for so long. Now that the time had come, she was glowing.

And Arthur, he practically worshiped Anya. When he looked at her, his eyes lit up like diamonds. They only hesitated because he would have to give up the pack once he turned. After the venom had entered his system, he would cease to be a werewolf. Since the pack's system was so patriarchal, his dad wasn't exactly excited that both of his sons planned to become vampires. Arthur and Roy did have a younger sister, Darcey, who would be a temporary alpha. As soon as she married, the role would be passed to her husband. I did feel bad for her. If she didn't want to be disowned by her parents, she would have to marry a wolf. That left her dating pool rather limited.

My sisters had both managed to find happiness in their immortal lives. They didn't worry or hesitate. They truly did seem alive. It made me wonder if I wasn't dead after all. Perhaps to be alive, I simply had to start living.

But it wasn't about me. It was about him. James had told me what he wanted. I didn't want to keep telling him no. If there was anything I could do to give him some small bit of happiness, I wanted to do it. After all, if we really intended to be together, if this was serious, we didn't have much of a choice.

I heard footsteps in the hall before my door even opened. As soon as his scent wafted into the room, I knew it was him. A small smile crept onto my face.

His arms wrapped around me as he placed a soft kiss on my neck. I leaned back against him, letting him hold me.

"They told me you were in here," James whispered.

I turned around to place a small kiss on his lips. "Hmm."

"I missed you," he whispered.

The sweet scent of his blood was everywhere. It was strawberries and lemons, roses and lilacs. His heartbeat was steady and constant.

I smiled. "I missed you, too."

He took my hand and led me toward the sofa. Moments later, he pulled me onto his lap. I ruffled his hair, watching as his green eyes electrified from my touch.

He leaned back, exposing his neck. "Will you?" James asked. "I've been thinking about it all day."

I nodded. "First, there's something I want to ask you."

He ran a hand through my hair. "Anything."

For a moment, the world seemed to stand still. This was it. I had never asked anyone a more heart-wrenching question. His answer would determine so much.

I took a deep breath. "Do you really want me to change you?"

His eyes lit up. "Yes."

I nodded. If he was sure, who was I to stop him? I knew he loved me and that I loved him. And after knowing what it felt like to be truly loved, I wasn't willing to give it up. No, I wouldn't lose him.

I sighed. "Okay."

He looked at me, stunned. "You mean you will?"

Yes, I would. He would be mine forever, and I would be his. Our future would be assured. Never again would I feel the loneliness I had felt for so long.

I stroked his cheek. "Yes."

His eyes grew wide. "Now."

"What?" I asked.

"Now," he demanded.

He pulled me toward him, tilting his head to the side. I tried to pull away, but his arms were wrapped around my back. His breathing was heavy in anticipation.

"I'm ready," he whispered.

"Oh, don't be ridiculous," I replied.

He looked at me in confusion. "What do you mean?"

"You're not ready," I replied. "You need an alibi, a new ID, all kinds of stuff like that. Not to mention you'll have to say goodbye to your family. I mean, we haven't even talked about that—"

"We'll figure all that out later," he interjected. "We're doing this, now."

"James...." I protested.

He looked into my eyes and wrapped his arms around my waist. "Now, before you change your mind."

I sighed. "Fine."

He smiled. "I love you, no matter what."

"I love you, too," I whispered.

A moment later, my fangs were in his neck. If this was going to be the last time I bit him as a human, I was going to enjoy it. I'd get a good bite before I gave him my venom. He laughed as I leaned in closer.

"I want you to have fun with this," he whispered.

I tangled my fingers in his hair, tilting his head farther to the side. He gasped, his fingers tightening around my waist.

"Take as much as you want," he mumbled. "It's

the last time you'll be able to."

I did. I took every last drop of sweetness that I wanted. The energy was flowing through my veins as I engulfed more and more. The intoxication was almost overwhelming.

"Did you do it yet?" James asked.

"Not yet," I breathed.

"Shh," he whispered. "Take your time."

Every time another drop flicked onto my tongue, sensation consumed me. I was acutely aware of every inch of his body. His breath, his heart, his lungs, I could feel all of them.

I'd been so consumed with him that I hadn't even heard the knock on the door. Nina burst into the room, panic flooding her eyes.

She caught her breath at first but recovered moments later. "Sorry to interrupt, but we have a situation."

I pulled away from him, blood trickling down my lips. Nina glanced between us before looking down at the floor.

She bit her lip. "Sorry, I didn't realize you were —"

"It's fine," I interrupted. I licked the blood from my lip before grabbing a tissue and handing it to James. "Here, use this."

He reached up to touch his neck. "You didn't get to it, did you?"

I pulled him off the couch. "No, I was just about

to. I'm sorry."

It was true. I had only been moments away from changing him. If she had been ten seconds later, the venom would have already been spreading through his veins.

He looked a little disappointed but nodded.

Nina glanced back at me. "We need to hurry."

I took his hand and led him to the door. "We're coming."

Chapter 13
Run

I held the bloody note in my shaking hands. Nina had already rushed around the apartment, locking all of the doors and windows, as well as pulling the black-out curtains closed. Anya was sitting on the couch, staring at the wall in shock. James was sitting beside her, not sure of what to do. They were both stunned.

I opened the note again, reading it for a second time.

We know what you're planning to do, you bloodsucking leach. You're all disgusting parasites ruining everything you touch. But guess what, we'll just kill you before you kill him. Our alpha deserves better than a bloodsucking Jezebel. You're dead, but this time for good.

Fists pounded on the door, causing us all to flinch. I just about dropped the blood-splattered letter in fear. Nina carefully opened the door, allowing Roy and Arthur to slip inside. Roy kissed her quickly before following Arthur over to where Anya was sitting on the couch.

Arthur cradled Anya in his arms, holding her tightly against him. "It's all right. I won't let anything happen to you," he whispered.

Her head was buried in his chest. "I'm scared."

He kissed the top of her head. "I know."

Roy walked back over toward me. "Can I see that?"

I nodded before handing him the note. He glanced over it quickly before lifting it to his nose. I watched his eyes as he registered the scent.

"It's wolf blood," he said.

"I know. I smelled it too," Nina confirmed.

"Well, we don't have to think very hard about who it is," I mumbled.

Arthur nodded, still holding Anya in his arms. "The question is how many wolves Pansy has recruited. We don't know how much of the pack is on her side."

"So, what will we do?" Nina asked. "There's no way we can know for sure. Obviously, none of them would tell you the truth."

James was watching the conversation with a mixture of fear and awe on his face. This was just about the last thing I wanted him involved in, not while he was still human. But if I let him out of my sight, he would become a liability. Pansy knew he was important to me, and she would use any sort of underhanded tactic she could to get what she wanted. She wanted Arthur, and she didn't care who she hurt to get to him.

"She'll never stop," Anya whispered.

Arthur tilted her chin up toward him. "I will not let her hurt you."

"I don't want you to get hurt," she whispered.

"Don't worry about that," Roy said. "Pansy won't touch him. Even if she's convinced some of the pack to take her side against you, there's no way they would agree to hurt him."

"There's an easy solution," Arthur replied. He glanced down at Anya before continuing. "Just change me."

She bit her lip. "If I do that, they'll expect Roy to take your place. When he doesn't, they'll go after Nina."

"Okay," Roy replied, "so change me, too. We were already planning on it." He looked over at Nina. "I know you didn't want to do it before the wedding, but we don't have much of a choice."

Arthur's eyes grew wide, but he didn't comment. James shot me a quick glance. Neither of them had known about the wedding. This probably wasn't the way Roy and Nina had envisioned telling them, but things had just gotten a whole lot more complicated.

Nina nodded. "You're right. The wedding can wait."

Roy and Arthur quickly glanced at each other. I could only imagine what they were feeling. This was a nightmare for all of us, but it was even worse for them.

Their family had turned against them. The pack, the people they had grown up with, had betrayed their trust.

"That settles things then," Roy said.

He took Nina's hand, leading her toward her bedroom. She shook her head, glancing at the fridge.

"It'll take days for the change to happen. We don't have enough blood for the three of us for those days, no less the two of you when you wake up," she said.

Anya bit her lip. "You're right. We need blood, a lot of it."

I pursed my lips. "I can get it."

They both looked at me and simultaneously asked, "Where?"

I sighed. "Albert."

Everyone looked uneasy but silently accepted that it was our only option. This was uncomfortable for everyone, but even more so for me. After all, I had just rejected one of the most powerful vampires in the world for a teenage boy from Georgia with pretty green eyes. I looked insane. There wasn't any way for me to explain it to Albert. He just couldn't understand. But maybe, just maybe, I would be able to convince him to help us.

"Even if all of this works perfectly, we need to get out of here, at least for right now," Nina said.

"You're right. It's not safe to stay here, not until this blows over," Anya agreed.

"Where will you go?" James asked with panic in his voice.

"Our safe-house outside Dallas," Nina answered.

James looked at me, his eyes filled with anxiety. "I'm going with you."

I nodded. "I know."

Even though the last place I wanted him to be was running from a pack of crazy werewolves with my family, I didn't have much choice in the matter. If he stayed in Savannah, Pansy would find him. It didn't leave me with very many options. This was the life he had chosen. We would just have to figure out something to tell his parents.

Nina looked concerned. "Anne, are you sure? Having a human around with two newly changed vampires might not be the best idea."

Our eyes locked in a glance that spoke volumes. "We'll need blood for six."

Everyone except James seemed a little surprised by my statement, but we didn't have time to worry about explanations. We would have to do the cleanup work later.

"Well, time to get packing," Nina said as she broke the silence.

"Anne, can you take care of the blood?" Anya confirmed.

"Yes," I replied.

"Okay." Nina glanced at each of us. "Let's try to be out of here in twenty-four hours."

Everyone began to disperse. Nina went to our

hidden safe underneath the floorboards to retrieve several spare passports, driver's licenses, and other IDs. Of course, they were all fake. Anya rummaged through the kitchen drawers in search of our backup credit cards and stacks of cash. Roy and Arthur began digging through a hidden compartment under Nina's bed that they had stocked with knives, bullets, and guns. We had to be prepared for these types of things. If we weren't, we would end up dead.

James pulled me to the side, lacing his fingers through mine. "I have to make up a story for my parents," he said. "If I disappear without telling them anything, it'll be bad."

I placed a soft kiss on his lips. "Okay, I'll take you. I don't want you going out alone. It's not safe. Besides, I have to stop to get the blood anyway."

He pulled me against him, wrapping his arms around my back. "It's all going to be okay. Soon, I'll be just like you."

I focused briefly on his heartbeat. Every single beat was like a flawless melody. Each time he took a breath, I could feel the strength of his powerful lungs. The blush in his cheeks, taste of his lips, and scent of his skin were all simply descriptions of his mortality.

"I know," I whispered. "Trust me, I know."

Chapter 14
A Girl

After dropping James off at his parents' house, I drove to Albert's apartment complex-turned-vampire-nest. As I walked up to the front door of the massive Victorian-style building, anxiety rose up in my chest. If I'd had a beating heart, I was positive it would have been pounding against my porcelain skin.

The building had been created and designed by Albert. He'd been born and grown up in Victorian England and had never quite moved away from the details of his childhood culture. The building was ridiculously tall, with many elaborate windows and several balconies. A majority of the lower floors held numerous small apartments for individual vampires or sometimes couples. Most of them worked for Albert in one of his numerous businesses. The upper floors had communal living areas, lounges, a private blood bar, and even a spacious ballroom. Albert's fortress-like home was legendary among vampires from all over the world.

It was one of the largest vampire dens in America and certainly the nicest.

Albert lived in the penthouse of the mansion-like residence. Many women had been rumored to visit the suite. Albert was a highly coveted prize, though he never seemed to keep any one woman around for very long. Most of them were passionate, week-long romances that quickly faded into memory. That was something I would never be content with.

My skin-tight black dress and ankle-strap pumps drew lots of attention as I stepped through the heavy wooden doors. I walked right into what appeared to be a large sitting room. A shiny chandelier hung from the ceiling, placing a gentle glow on the wooden floors and plush, red sofas. The black walls only added to the intimidating atmosphere. It felt like I was entering a palace.

A few female vampires were scattered around the room, whispering to each other in tones too soft to hear. They were beautiful. Dressed in evening gowns with glasses of chilled blood in their hands, the female vampires were terrifying and glamorous. I felt small in comparison.

Male vampires, most with haughty expressions on their faces, were playing a game of poker. They looked like businessmen who had gone out for a drink after work and gotten a little carried away. I would have been nervous to speak to them.

They all stared at me as I walked past them toward the large elevators. As soon as the doors had shut behind me, I breathed a sigh of relief. There was a reason I had chosen my sisters over groups like this. These vampires were downright scary, and I certainly didn't want to make a bad impression. Living in this den would be like eternal high school, simply terrible.

Finally, the elevator reached the top floor. I had expected to step directly into Albert's apartment but found myself in a small waiting room instead. There was a large wooden desk with a woman sitting behind it. She didn't look up at me but instead kept filling out an extremely large stack of paperwork. Her shiny, golden name tag read "Kara."

"Um, excuse me," I said.

She glanced up at me, tucking her wavy brown hair behind her ears. She was rather small, probably shorter than me, with a thin frame. Her eyelashes bloomed above her sparkling eyes.

"Yes?" Kara asked.

"I need to speak with Albert," I replied.

She gave me a rather confused look before standing and walking to a door on the far side of the room. She knocked loudly on the heavy door. A feeling of anxiety overwhelmed me as I waited.

"Mr. Jefferson," she said, "there's a girl here to see you."

His deep voice was loud enough that I could still

hear it from all the way across the room. "Is it one of the girls from Clovers? If it is, tell her I'm busy."

I inwardly cringed. Clovers was a well-known private werewolf gentlemen's club. I glanced down at myself. I was wearing a tight black dress, but it wasn't exactly scandalous. It was knee-length! Kara, wearing her purple skirt-suit, glanced back at me.

"No, sir," she replied, "she's a vampire." Her eyes met mine. "What's your name?"

"Anne Emerson," I replied.

Kara turned back toward the door. "It's a Miss Anne Emerson, sir."

The door flew open, almost knocking Kara over. She glanced at Albert in shock.

Albert's hair was wet, plastered to his neck. His dark eyes were filled with a pleasant surprise. His dress shirt was halfway unbuttoned, revealing a bit of his marble chest.

He gave me a genuine smile. "Anne!"

I hadn't expected to find him so cheerful. Actually, I'd never seen Albert in such a rawly-good mood. It was slightly odd but a pleasant surprise.

I smiled back. "Hi."

He positioned the door wide open. "Come on in."

I walked inside, glad to be out of the awkward waiting room.

Before he shut the door, I heard him say, "Kara, tell everyone I'm busy. I don't care who calls. I'm occupied.

No interruptions."

Despite her perplexed stare, she nodded. That must be an incredibly hard job, I thought to myself. Albert had to be a very strange person to work for. I couldn't even imagine what being his secretary would have been like.

Moments later, I heard the door firmly shut behind us. The wide living room was decorated beautifully. The dark wooden floors were a lovely combination with the soft, cream-colored walls. Antique red-velvet couches added some warm color to the room. There was a large bookshelf built into the wall, a desk with stationery, and another door that appeared to lead into a bedroom. Nineteenth-century paintings decorated the large room. Hanging from the ceiling was a huge chandelier adorned with real, flickering candles. On the far side of the room were French doors which opened to a large, moonlit balcony where a German shepherd rested.

I hadn't known what to expect, but this was far prettier than I had imagined. The room smelled of rosewood, creating a home-like feel. It was a relaxing space.

Through the door to his bedroom, I saw a huge, kingsize, four-poster bed with plush velvet covers. Black carpet covered the floor, creating a cozy feel. For a moment, I thought about what it would be like to be in that room. I quickly shook the thoughts from my mind.

Albert motioned to one of the couches, still smiling. "Sit."

The soft cushions seemed to melt beneath me. I was tempted to slip off my heels and relax, but then I remembered why I was there. Albert gently sat down beside me, resting his arm on the couch above my shoulders. I thought about scooting away but decided against it. From where we were sitting, we had a beautiful view of the moon. It was hard to believe that only hours ago, I had been preparing to turn James into an immortal. But then, chaos erupted.

"So what brings you here by the light of the moon, beautiful?" His dark eyes bored into mine.

I could try to distract him, to break it to him softly, but I couldn't bring myself to do it. There was no point in hiding my intentions. Albert would find out the truth eventually.

I sighed. "To be honest, I need to ask you for something."

A small smile crept onto his lips. "Whatever you want."

My hands began to shake, so I clasped them together to hide my nervousness. "I need blood."

He grinned. "Well, that I can definitely give."

Albert leaned over, beginning to pull me toward him. I gently took his arms from around me and laid them down. The brightness from his eyes immediately vanished. It was as if they had gone from sparkling midnight jewels to deep black holes.

"That's not what I meant," I whispered.

He nodded, clearly disappointed. "You need packets?"

I smiled in gratitude. "Yes, thank you."

He walked over toward the door, quickly opening it and saying, "Kara, I need enough blood for three brought up in coolers. Make it plenty for a month, please."

"Um, Albert," I whispered.

He glanced back at me.

I pushed the nervousness from my mind as I attempted to harness my courage. This wasn't a question I wanted to ask. But I had to; my family was counting on me.

"Do you think you could make it enough for six, please?" I asked in a nervous tone.

A sick feeling flooded through my stomach as I waited for his reaction. He would know what I was doing. He would be disappointed, maybe even angry. I didn't want to make him feel that way.

He seemed perplexed, but then realization flooded his eyes. "Anne, what are you doing?"

"We have to leave. The pack is turning on Arthur," I replied.

He nodded. "Okay, I understand that. But why are you taking blood for the human? Actually, why are you taking him at all?"

"I can't just leave him," I replied.

There was a moment of silence. His eyes were locked in conversation with mine. Our souls were speaking. Whether I liked it or not, there was something deep within me communicating with him.

"Anne, he's a human. He doesn't belong in this. And even if you're planning on changing him, have you thought about how much more complicated you're going to make this situation? Having two new vampires will be challenging enough. You certainly don't need a third to deal with."

My eyes were becoming watery. "If I leave James, the wolves will come for him."

Albert groaned. "Humans are so problematic."

I rolled my eyes. "You used to be one, too."

He gave me a sad smile. "I know, and I can't express to you how difficult it was."

I was silent for a moment. I somewhat knew who Albert was—everyone did. He was a vampire celebrity, almost a monarch. Everyone knew he'd always been rich beyond belief, both before and after he had become an immortal. He had grown up in Victorian England, something he was quite proud of. In fact, he had what appeared to be an original portrait of the young Queen Victoria displayed in his ballroom. It was something everyone who attended his galas knew. I'd been to a few of them only because Nina had insisted.

But I had never heard what happened to him. I had no idea how a handsome, rich bachelor had ended up becoming one of the most well-known vampires in the world. There was a part of me that was incredibly curious.

"Why?" I asked in a soft voice.

He walked over and sat down beside me. Albert ran a hand through his messy hair, allowing it to fall down against his neck. His black-brown eyes contained sadness stronger than I'd ever imagined him experiencing. It almost broke my heart.

"My life was relatively perfect until 1864. I was twenty-three and one of the most eligible bachelors in London. Though I had no interest in marrying. I was far too attached to my drinking, gambling, and late-night trips to the brothels."

He paused for a moment, examining my wide eyes. "Eventually, my parents decided they wanted grandchildren. Or, more specifically, a grandson. And so, fathers of pretty girls practically flocked to my mother. They would introduce their daughters as the finest in the country. Many of them were truly beautiful. I didn't deny that. But I turned most of them away. I was bored with the very concept of marriage. After a while, my parents got so frustrated that they picked a girl for me. Before I even knew about the arrangement, I had been promised to her. Of course, I couldn't reject her at that point. The poor girl would have been mortified. So with reluctance, I accepted."

He paused again, taking a deep breath before continuing. "The moment I met her, all of my anxieties vanished. She was a small, pale-skinned girl with pretty gray eyes and deep red lips. Her light blonde hair and gentle smile made her seem like a real-life Cinderella. She must have known about my horrendous reputation because when I smiled at her, her cheeks turned crimson. Her name was Flora."

His face was free from all expression as he relished in the memory. "I happily agreed to a hastily planned wedding. As our engagement continued, Flora grew more comfortable around me. Eventually, we developed a strange sort of friendship. I would flatter her, and she would become flustered. No matter how many times I saw her smile, it wasn't enough. My parents were just thrilled that I'd finally calmed down. Everyone was perfectly content with the marriage arrangements. Things relaxed for a while as I began to settle into my new life."

He froze for a second, taking a moment to collect himself. "A week before our wedding, Flora, our parents, my sister, and I were leaving a late-night dinner party. The rain poured down as our carriages sloshed through the wet London streets. I'm not sure how it happened, but something must have scared the horses. We crashed, and my sister, Hazel, and I were the only ones left alive. Both of us were badly injured, and we would have died if we hadn't been bitten. A man, or rather a vampire, who happened to own one of the bars that I had frequented, stumbled upon us. He saved Hazel and I."

I looked at him in absolute horror. This wasn't anything like I'd imagined. We'd grown up in completely different places and times, but we'd suffered similar fates. We'd both lost our first love to tragedy.

I didn't know what to say. How could I communicate the sheer empathy I felt? I knew how his heart had broken. Mine had done the same.

"Hazel and I disappeared from London," Albert said. "Everyone accepted our absence. After all, we were in mourning. We went to Vienna for a while, then to Dublin. Eventually, Hazel wanted to return to London. And so, decades after we'd left, we returned with new names and stories. We still had our family's wealth, which was exceedingly helpful. Still, I ended up making my way to America. It satisfied me, so I've lived here ever since. I still have a place in London, and I go to visit my sister frequently. But even though I visit, I could never live there again."

I had no idea how to respond. What was the appropriate response to such a story? There was nothing I could think to say that would express the level of compassion in my heart. He'd suffered as I had. To live with those types of memories was horrifying.

"I'm sorry," I whispered.

He stroked my cheek. "I don't want you to be sorry. I want you to know that I love you, and I want you. I'm right for you, Anne. We understand each other."

I felt as if I was suffocating. Was he right? It seemed a likely possibility. Perhaps he truly did understand me. His story tore my heart apart.

But even so, I couldn't go along with it. I'd given my heart to James. I couldn't turn my back on him. It wouldn't be fair. Besides, it really wasn't a choice. James was my everything, my world wrapped in the fragile shell of a human. Giving him up would be like surrendering the very ground beneath my feet. It wasn't possible if I wanted to maintain even a small bit of happiness.

A knock sounded on the door. "Mr. Jefferson," Kara said, "it's here."

He stood up, walking over to the door and opening it to reveal three coolers of packaged blood. It was more than I could have expected. Albert was a lot of things I didn't care to think about, but he was generous. That was something I was sure of.

I stood and walked to the door. There were two men holding the coolers, waiting to follow me out.

"I have to go," I whispered.

He sighed, exhaustion clearly showing on his face. "I know."

"Thank you, Albert. Really, it means a lot," I said.

He watched me for a few moments before replying. "Just know, Anne, if you fall apart, I'll be here to pick up the pieces."

And with that, he gently shut his door.

Chapter 15

BLOODLUST

I drove faster than I'd ever driven in my life. It was a small attempt to control my shaking hands. The coolers in the back of the car slid into the doors as I cut quickly to the right. Luckily, few people were on the road in the middle of the night.

I slid into our apartment building's parking lot as if I was trying to escape a herd of stampeding elephants. Going as fast as I could, I left the coolers in the car before hurrying up to our apartment. I was the first one back. Nina and Roy had gone to collect a few things from his place, Arthur and Anya were at his parents' house explaining the situation, and James was still where I'd left him. As soon as my sisters came back with the boys, we'd go pick up James and start our drive to the safe house.

I practically sprinted up to the apartment to throw a bag of my things together before we left. After pulling it out of my purse, I slid the key into the lock before opening the door.

As soon as I stepped inside, I froze in shock. The whole room was covered in blood. The furniture lay broken and battered on the floor, the windows were shattered, and the walls were streaked with blood. I walked over, quickly touching my finger to the wall before bringing it up to my nose. I sighed in relief—at least it was animal blood.

With hesitation, I walked back into the other rooms in the apartment. Everything was destroyed. Still, on guard, I went into my room last to find another blood-stained note laying on the floor. My hands shook with anxiety as I opened it, spilling blood all over my palms. I was in so much shock that the scent of the fresh blood didn't even bother me. My terror heavily outweighed my thirst.

You made a mistake, leach. Leaving your pet all alone was the worst thing you could have done. And now, he's mine. After all, it's only fair. You take ours, and we take yours. We won't allow ourselves to be controlled by lifeless, bloodthirsty creatures of the night. Werewolves have, and always will be, more than that. We're stronger than you, and we're going to prove it. For every drop of blood your sisters take from them, I'll take ten of his. And by the end of it, he'll be dead.

I fell to the ground, the letter tumbling to the floor. If I had been a human, I probably would have passed out.

But I was a vampire—I didn't have that luxury. Pansy had James. I had no idea how she'd found him, but she had. All of my worst fears about leaving him alone had materialized. I never should have let him out of my sight, I thought to myself.

I wasn't sure how long I sat there rereading the letter over and over again. I tried to think, but the panic was too strong. My throat was tight. It was almost the same sensation I had when I was thirsty, but this was from dread.

I imagined all of the horrible things they might do to him. Regardless of what the legends said, werewolves could be just as cruel as vampires. They could kill and destroy just as much as us. Like most vampires, they usually didn't. But as with all types of creatures, there were evil ones. Pansy was one of them. She would go to almost any lengths to get what she wanted. But she was even angrier than usual because she knew she was losing. This wasn't some sort of clever tactic to try to convince Arthur and Roy to change their minds. It wasn't a threat to scare us away. No, this was merciless revenge.

Arthur had always been able to control her. He had kept her in line, but he had never attempted to micromanage. Most of the pack appreciated their freedom. Many of the wolves were capable of governing themselves. But of course, Pansy had never had that type of maturity. She, along with a few others, had always been wild. Arthur had spent most of his time as alpha lecturing them, making sure they fixed whatever disasters they caused.

But when he had started dating Anya, things had begun to spiral. Wolves had started turning against him, and the pack had become hostile. Then, there had been the alpha challenge from Dale. Of course, Arthur had won. But in many ways, it had only increased the tension within the pack. Now, Pansy had managed to radicalize enough wolves to start a rebellion. Well, more of a sabotage.

But somehow, James had gotten wrapped up in it. And it was all my fault. *This is what you get for dating a human,* I thought to myself. Every inch of my body was rigid with fear. Terror coursed through my veins. He was probably petrified. I didn't have any idea where he was or how to find him. What was I supposed to do?

I had no idea how long I had been sitting on the floor. My mind had been going a million miles an hour. Eventually, I heard a distant scream. But I didn't move. I was practically frozen from shock.

Nina and Anya were screaming my name. Moments later, they burst into my room. They rushed over toward me, wrapping me in their arms.

"What happened?!" Nina asked.

"Are you all right?!" Anya cried.

Nina's eyes floated to the note laying in front of me. She picked it up, opening its blood-stained folds. I watched her eyes widen as she examined it. She brought it up to her nose, sniffing it. Nina visibly relaxed and moved it away from her face.

"What is it?" Anya asked.

"It's animal blood," Nina replied.

Anya let out a sigh of relief. I had already known it wasn't his blood. If it had been, I would have smelled it long before I brought it to my nose. His scent was unmistakable.

But just because it wasn't his blood didn't mean Pansy hadn't hurt him. All it meant was that she hadn't hurt him yet. Who knew how long it had been since she had left the note? By now, he could be dead.

Nina handed the note to Roy, who was standing behind her. Once he'd read it, he passed it to Arthur. Their faces were grim. We all knew just how sadistic Pansy was. She would torture him and enjoy every moment of it. She was just that crazy.

"Can you find her?" Anya asked Arthur.

He nodded. "I can follow her scent. It shouldn't be too hard to pick up."

Roy took my hand and pulled me from the ground. My legs felt wobbly as I struggled to stand on my own. Roy held my arms, steadying me.

"Anne, are you okay?" Roy asked.

"I'll be fine," I whispered.

He nodded. "Will you be all right coming with us?"

I pursed my lips in determination. "If she hurts

him, she's dead."

Arthur nodded. "Agreed."

We began walking toward the door as my phone rang. For a moment, a spark of hope dashed through my chest. It was James. I quickly answered the phone, bringing it to my ear.

"So," Pansy's sickening voice began. "I assume you got my letter."

She giggled in a crazed manner. She must have been a real, true psychopath. In another life, perhaps she could have been a serial killer.

"Where is he?" I spoke through clenched teeth.

Never before had I wanted to sink my fangs into someone so badly. I wanted to obliterate her. I would never be satisfied until I saw her experience every ounce of pain she'd caused James. It seemed impossible, but I detested her even more than the monster who had taken my human life away.

"Oh, he's enjoying our time together," she replied.

Her disgusting, high-pitched laugh made me want to scream. Every inch of my body was shaking. The tension in my fist continued to build. Nina laid her hand on my shoulder. I relaxed slightly, but the anxiety in my stomach was still overflowing.

"If you touch him, I'll kill you," I hissed.

"Don't be so dramatic," she replied.

It took so much effort to prevent myself from screaming. My throat was practically burning from the unquenchable desire to tear her apart. This wolf had pushed me to my limits, and it wouldn't be long before she had to deal with the consequences.

Arthur took the phone out of my shaking hand. "Pansy. I'm only going to ask once. Stop this."

With my ultra-sensitive hearing, I could hear her anger-filled reply.

"You've ruined everything for us. Thanks to you, we'll be left without a real alpha. And the worst part, it's all because you fell in love with a sick, trampy bloodsucker," Pansy replied.

He took a deep breath before replying, "You've made a mistake."

I could hear the challenge in her voice just before she hung up the phone. "We'll see."

He handed my phone back with a grim look on his face. "It's time to go."

Chapter 16
My Everything

I sat in the back while Arthur and Anya were in front. Roy and Nina were in the car behind us. We were speeding through the streets as if we were trying to outrun a tornado, but I didn't really notice. All I could hear was my own unsteady breathing.

Briefly, I glanced out the window at the rising sun. It didn't seem beautiful at all, only menacing. Each moment that passed was another when I wasn't with James. As the sun continued to climb higher, so did his misery.

Each time I closed my eyes, all I could see was James's face in absolute agony. I envisioned Pansy with a sick grin on her lips as she placed hundreds of small cuts all over his soft skin. The blood trickled down his body, creating a pool beneath him. I couldn't help but think that was what he would look like when we arrived. Or maybe it would be even worse than I had imagined—he might already be dead.

Every breath I took seemed to stop in my throat. It was like a nightmare, except it was real. All of this disaster had happened so quickly. One moment, it had just been the two of us. If we'd had a few more seconds, I would have turned him. Then, of course, the transformation would have taken days. But at least we wouldn't have been in this situation.

I never should have let him out of my sight. He would have been safe with me. Why hadn't I just taken him with me? Any confrontation between him and Albert would have been better than this. I'd just been too stupid to think about it. I had thought he would be safe for a few hours within the walls of his own home. He had wanted time with his parents. It had been such a simple request. I had failed him in every way possible.

Whether or not we got there before it was too late, I would kill Pansy myself. Then, I would change him. I wasn't going to wait any longer. I had already delayed it once, and look where it had gotten me. Now I was giving him my venom as soon as I had the chance. I refused to lose James. And leaving him human was too risky.

The car lurched sideways as Arthur darted back and forth between cars. He hadn't let me drive. It was probably a good thing; my hands were still shaking.

"Turn here!" Anya yelled.

I fell against the door as the car made a hard right.

I could hear Nina and Roy speeding behind us. We had to go faster. We had to make it in time. If we didn't,

I had no idea what I would do.

"Faster," I urged.

Arthur accelerated, pushing the car to its limit. Still, it wasn't fast enough.

What if we were too late? What if he was already dead? He would have died knowing I hadn't been able to save him. And it would all be my fault. All of this because I'd fallen in love with a human. Why had I even done it? Because he's exactly what you wanted when you were seventeen, I thought.

I envisioned his gorgeous emerald eyes. They were more entrancing than any crystal ball I'd ever seen. And his soft blond hair, it was like silk. The way his arms wrapped around me was like waves embracing the sand. Our lips blended perfectly together like sugar and tea. If my heart had a beat, it would have been the same as his.

But if he died, would I be able to live with myself? No, probably not. I would hate myself for the rest of eternity. This immortal life would become even more miserable. No matter how hard I tried, I would never be able to forget him.

"We're almost there, Anne," Arthur said. His voice was gentle. "Just try to hold on. He'll need you when we get there."

"What if it's too late?" I whispered.

Anya turned around, her eyes meeting mine. "It won't be."

I nodded, hoping she was right.

We drove farther and farther until I felt as if I might scream from anxiety. Every second it took us to get there was another second he was in pain, another second Pansy had her hands on him, another second before I could rip her apart. My fangs were aching to burst from my mouth. First to kill her, and second to change him.

What seemed like hours but was actually moments later, we pulled up to a small gray house separated from the road by a huge expanse of trees. It stood alone with no other buildings in sight. I hadn't even noticed when we'd left the main road. I wasn't nearly as focused as I needed to be.

We practically jumped out of the car, running up to the house as if we were doing a military raid. I was still wearing my dress and pumps. My heels clicked on the ground as I rushed to the door. There wasn't a plan; we weren't organized, but we knew exactly what we needed to do.

Arthur kicked the door open with his werewolf strength, and we flooded the room. It was dark and wet — the house smelled as if it had been empty for years. I glanced around the room quickly, and then I saw her. For a brief moment, Pansy's face registered panic and shock. But then her sick, sadistic grin returned. She was sitting on the ground, James underneath her.

He looked barely conscious. Blood oozed from the innumerable cuts all over his body. Pansy held a dagger in her hand. She'd been carving his body like a piece of meat.

I wanted to run to him, to pull him into my arms. I wanted to change him right then and there. But I couldn't because I had to deal with her first. Luckily, there were only three of them: Pansy, Dale, and another wolf I recognized as her boyfriend.

The two boys were standing at attention, looking as if they would shift at any moment. But before they had a chance, Roy and Arthur were on top of them. Roy snapped Pansy's boyfriend's neck without a moment of hesitation. Mercy wasn't involved in this equation. This was a kill or be killed situation; we had no other choice.

Pansy let out a soft yelp of pain before abandoning James and dashing toward the door.

"Pansy!" Dale cried.

She ignored him, running full force toward the exit. But before she had a chance to escape, Nina tackled her to the floor. Pansy screamed in pain as her head hit the hard, stone ground. Nina glanced at me as I began walking toward her.

I stood before Pansy, staring directly into her eyes. She looked crazed and furious. She doesn't even care that she's going to die, I thought to myself. Her light hair was plastered to her neck with sweat. Her face was splattered with blood, and her shirt was torn and covered in dirt. She didn't seem to care; her deranged spirit was too lost to register a proper amount of terror.

My eyes were locked with Pansy's. I was fully

aware that I was staring at the one who had tried to murder the man I loved. Knowledge like that allowed for a new, sharper kind of hate. It wasn't superficial or petty. No, this was pure fury.

Anya stood behind me with her hand on my shoulder. Pansy had stopped struggling beneath Nina and instead let out a maniacal laugh. Her eyes seemed to catch fire as I hissed, my fangs protruding from my lips.

In that moment, I was consumed with rage. Perhaps some would have called me crazy or even disturbed. Maybe they would have thought me cruel. But even so, wasn't there someone everyone would kill for? Didn't we all have a lover, child, or friend we would destroy for? And not even that, but wouldn't we all avenge someone we loved? She had made the decision to hurt him, and so I would make her burn.

Nina glanced at me again as I knelt down so that my face was only inches from Pansy's. I could smell her wolf blood flowing through her veins, but it didn't appeal to me. I was too repulsed to be tempted. Her blood wasn't sweet like James's. No, it smelled dirty and diluted. Not because she was a wolf, but because of how much disgust I held for her.

"I hate you, you filthy leach," Pansy hissed.

I tilted my head to the side, my fangs slipping and slicing open my lip. "I know."

Half a second later, my fangs sunk into her neck. She let out a small cry of pain before collapsing onto the ground. Realizing Pansy no longer posed a threat, Nina rose to stand beside Anya. They watched with a sort of contentment in their eyes as the blood drained from Pansy's body.

It took strength to consume her blood. Unlike any blood I had ever tasted, it was completely repulsive. I didn't want to taste it. It was like spoiled milk, absolutely disgusting. But still, I drained her as quickly as possible.

It only took a few minutes before her body collapsed into a lifeless heap. I stood, wiping her blood from my mouth with my sleeve. The horrible taste was still in my mouth, but I didn't care. This was what I had wanted. She had paid for what she'd done to James. That was what mattered.

I turned around to see Dale's corpse collapsed on the ground. I hadn't even noticed when they'd killed him. Arthur or Roy must have taken care of it. Then I heard a soft cry of anguish escape James's lips.

"Anne," he whispered with pain-filled eyes.

I darted toward him, collapsing on the ground beside his wounded body. Roy and Arthur were already there, attempting to bandage his wounds as quickly as possible. Nina and Anya joined them, ripping pieces of cloth and tying them around the gashes in his legs.

"You better hurry, Anne," Nina whispered. "He's going fast."

Panic rushed through me as I laid down beside him. I took his bloody hand in my own, but he didn't even seem to notice. He was in too much pain to care what was happening. My heart seemed to shatter. I was falling apart. This was one of the most terrible things I had ever witnessed. Nothing in my immortal life had been more challenging to see than this. It felt as if I was crumbling on the inside.

I could barely speak. "It's okay," I mumbled into his ear. "I'm going to take care of you."

And with that, I gently placed my fangs within his neck. I wasn't even sure if he registered what was happening—he seemed too unaware. But still, I hoped the venom would give him some bit of pleasure, maybe even take a bit of the pain away.

His sweet blood wiped the taste of Pansy's from my mouth. It was as subtle as lavender and vanilla but as unmistakable as cinnamon and honey. I wanted more, more, and more. It was hard to even stop for a moment to release my venom, but I did. I pumped as much of it as I could into his bloodstream, careful to let his body absorb it before I kept drinking. The more his body received, the faster his transformation would be; his pain would vanish quicker.

As soon as I was sure he had absorbed the venom, I began drinking again. It didn't matter how much he lost at this point—he had already started to change. Within moments the pain from his wounds seemed to disappear. The venom had spread far enough to begin binding his cuts from the inside out.

It seemed as if that moment lasted forever. His contentment and my blissfulness consumed us. He was floating, and I was soaring. He began to let out soft gasps as his body was consumed with relaxation. *Good*, I thought. I couldn't bear the idea of him being in pain any longer.

Eventually, I became so full that I had to stop. I moved away from his neck, pulling him up into my arms. Everyone seemed to relax; we had made it in time.

I tried to ignore the sickening sensation spreading through my stomach. It wouldn't be long before he was in pain again. Once the venom had healed his wounds, it would begin the actual change. His soft human skin would become rock-hard, and his heart would beat for the last time. James would be miserable until his change was complete.

I rocked his unconscious form within my arms. I had never held him so tightly before. Before tonight, I had always been afraid of breaking him; now, it didn't matter. Once he was changed, I could hold him as tightly as I wanted. I would never have to let him go. James would be mine forever. I wouldn't have to worry about killing him anymore. When I kissed him, I wouldn't have to think about bruising his lips. I'd finally be able to love him with every ounce of strength I possessed. But first, we had to survive these few miserable days.

"I love you so much, James. I'll never let you go again," I whispered.

I knew his mind couldn't hear me, but maybe his heart could. Or perhaps our souls were speaking to each other. Either way, I knew some part of him would be able to feel the love I was pouring out. And when James opened his immortal eyes for the first time, I would hold him against me and never stop telling him just how much I adored him.

I watched silently as Roy, Arthur, Nina, and Anya collected the bodies. They dragged them out into the woods, disposing of them as quickly as possible. Moments later, I detected the smell of burning flesh. It wouldn't be long before they were nothing more than ash. They'd be obliterated into dirt, disappearing into the winds of time. They would never be able to hurt anyone, steal a life, or destroy someone's love again.

It was over—this nightmare had come to an end. But now, a new one would begin. Soon, the pain would start. James would be consumed with misery as his body froze in time. He'd forever be a teenager, just like me. Both of us would be teenagers for the rest of our existence. But even so, I would never have to lose him. That was what was important.

"You're my everything," I whispered with my forehead pressed against his.

Soon, they all returned. Arthur took James from my arms, moving him to the car. I sat with his head on my lap, pretending he had fallen into a blissful sleep. My love was becoming like me. Soon, nothing would be able to separate us.

As Arthur began to drive, I fell into my thoughts. Losing James's humanity hadn't been nearly as hard as I had imagined. I had thought I would hate myself for stealing his innocence. That maybe he wouldn't be my James anymore. But no, when he woke, we would have forever to love each other. I would have eternity to give him my heart.

Anya smiled at me from the front seat. "He'll be okay, Anne."

I gave her a small smile in return. "I know."

Chapter 17

FREEZING

The first few hours of our trip were relatively silent, except for Snuffles persistent meowing. Eventually, Anya turned on some music. She played my favorite songs: "Clair de Lune," "Des pas sur la neige," and "Moonlight Sonata." I relaxed into them, allowing my mind to drift into the world of piano. There was something about the gentle notes that made me feel as if I was laying on a cloud. Their melancholy harmony was soothing.

As the sweet songs played on repeat, I stroked James's hair. My fingers curled within the soft strands of gold. I admired his thick lashes, plush lips, and strawberry blush. Light freckles that I'd never paid much attention to before dotted his nose. There was so much depth to him that it would probably take me all of forever to notice every single aspect of his beauty.

As time passed, he began to grow uncomfortable. I noticed the change when his heartbeat slowed. It didn't stop, but it was certainly on its way. His skin grew frigid.

I wanted to pull a blanket over him, but it wouldn't be of any use. His body was becoming frozen in place. As he made his transformation, the normal heat of his human form would vanish. For any normal person, this would have made them freeze to death. But for a soon-to-be-vampire, it was simply an indication that the transformation had truly begun. The cherry color had left his cheeks, leaving them to turn snow-white. He looked like he was dying; in a way, he was.

It was painful for me to watch his discomfort. I didn't want to see his pain. But even so, leaving him to suffer through it alone was unthinkable. Besides, we had to make it to Texas. We would be at the safe house before his transformation was complete. He would wake up on my daybed, seeing the world through his immortal eyes for the very first time. I hoped I was the first thing he saw. I wanted to be there to embrace him, to hold him against me until he was so thirsty he had to let go. James would start his new life, and I'd be there to guide him the entire way.

"How is he?" Arthur asked.

"Normal, I suppose," I replied.

"He looks freezing," Arthur commented.

"His body temperature is dropping. If he didn't have her venom, he'd be freezing to death," Anya replied.

Arthur's eyes widened in shock. In just a few days, he'd be in the same position James was in now. It only took a few moments for Arthur to recover. His eyes calmed as he relaxed into the reality of it.

"How long will it take?" Arthur asked.

Anya pursed her lips. "I'm not completely sure. Maybe four or five days. I don't have much experience with it, to be honest."

Arthur didn't look too panicked. He was so determined to spend forever with Anya that he probably would have climbed Mount Everest if it was required for his transformation. He was clearly a little nervous, which was entirely rational. But his fear certainly wasn't going to stop him. He had decided what he wanted to do with his life long ago.

"When do you think you'll change me?" Arthur asked Anya.

"Soon after we get there. I don't want to put it off for too long," she replied. Their fingers were laced together as she spoke. "Though, I do have a surprise." A huge grin spread across her face. "I've already contacted a justice of the peace. He agreed to meet us at the house. Nina deserves to have a wedding, even if it's not as big and beautiful as we'd planned. The dress should be there when we arrive, along with the flowers and decorations. I already arranged for someone to set it all up in the backyard. It won't be too elaborate, but at least it'll be something."

Arthur smiled, stroking her cheek. "You're right. I'm sure she'll be very happy."

I smiled to myself. *Good, Nina will have her wedding,*

I thought.

At least something was going well. Not much good had happened within the last few days, but this little wedding, which would likely just include us and the justice of the peace, would be a beam of sunshine illuminating the darkness. Maybe one day, when James had adjusted to immortality, we would have a wedding. I'd always wanted to be married. Many things had changed after I'd become a vampire, but my desire for marriage never had. It may have been buried for a while, but it had never disappeared.

We drove for hours upon hours. Eventually, Nina and Anya took over driving so the boys could sleep. After all, they'd been up all night. We never stopped for long, though. We were all anxious to get to the safe house. I hadn't been there in months. We paid an elderly werewolf woman to look after it, so it didn't seem abandoned in our absence. The three of us had decided to purchase it years ago in preparation for a situation like this. We knew there would come a time when we needed to escape Savannah, even if it was only for a little bit. In a few months, we would go back. We would have to call someone to fix our apartment, but after that, we could return to our strange, semi-normal life. This was only temporary.

I was immediately pulled away from my thoughts as I felt James's body shudder. He was frigid. I pulled him closer to me, cradling his head against my chest. His skin was already starting to stiffen. When it was over, he would be like me: hard as marble.

"Shh, love. It's all right. It'll be over soon," I whispered.

And for both our sakes, I hoped it would be. He shivered again, leaning into me. I ran my hands gently through his hair. Everything about him would harden — even his silky golden locks would become thicker and more firm. But when it was over, at least I could rest assured that no disease, car accident, or natural disaster could ever kill him. He'd finally be safe.

Anya's eyes met mine through the mirror. "I'll drive as fast as I can."

I gave her an appreciative smile. "Thank you."

She turned up the radio, allowing "Death by A Thousand Cuts" to resonate through the otherwise-silent vehicle. Taylor's voice echoed around me as I pulled James closer still.

Chapter 18

MARRIAGE

Our cream-colored, brick, ranch-style house looked like a cottage in the moonlight. Small lanterns decorated the wooden porch leading up to our medieval-looking door. The safe house was surrounded by cedar trees with a small stream flowing through the backyard. It was peaceful.

Arthur carried James inside, Roy following behind him with our bags. James was laid down on the daybed in my room. I sat beside him in my dimly lit, whitewashed sanctuary. Candles illuminated the space, emulating a soft light over James's pale face. The heavy drapes were pulled shut, sealing us from the outside world.

His skin had continued to transform into a marble masterpiece. His lashes were thicker, lips plumper and blood-red, and his nicely-toned muscles had solidified. I washed his body, gently cleaning away the blood that had dried on his skin. When I was finished, Arthur and Roy helped me change him into a black cotton shirt and pants. His clothes fell softly against his now stone-like chest. With every second, he seemed to be getting closer.

The process was almost ceremonial. I adjusted a vase full of roses on my vanity, filling the room with their sweet scent. The antique record player, which sat atop my large wooden desk, played soft, soothing music that put my mind at ease. And to prepare for when he woke up, I'd poured two glasses of chilled blood and adorned them with sweet-smelling cherries. More for myself than James, I'd also washed and arranged my curls in as orderly a fashion as I could manage and changed into a lavender floor-length dress. It was light and airy, framing my chest before falling down in gentle waves to the cool, stone floor. When James woke up, I wanted to be the first thing his ultra-sensitive eyes glimpsed.

As soon as the sun emerged from its sleep, Anya revealed her secret plans. She led Nina into the backyard, which had already been adorned with an arch made from magnolia blossoms and long, white ribbons. A small stone path extended from the French doors out into the grass where the arch was located. Nina squealed with excitement as she glimpsed the magical setting for the first time. She ran back into the house to retrieve Roy, dragging him out to glimpse the setting for himself. He smiled brightly as he watched her excitement. It was beautiful.

Anya and I helped Nina change into her wedding dress. It was a lace sweetheart gown that tightly gripped her chest and hips before falling down to burst into an explosion of ruffles around her thighs. The mermaid dress perfectly complemented her gorgeous figure, making her seem as if she were a heavenly creature.

Anya had changed into a tight, blush colored dress with a giant slit that reached the top of her thighs. Her heels shimmered as she spun around the room. As usual, she was lovely.

I still wore my lavender dress but had added a pair of golden stilettos to appear more formal. Together, the three of us looked like we were ready to take on the world.

"Are you anxious?" Anya asked.

"Not even a little," Nina replied.

She didn't seem nervous at all as she held her white hydrangea bouquet and stepped out into the sunshine in her sparkly pumps, making her way toward Roy. Anya and I walked on either side of her the whole way. Nina said it was only right that we accompanied her down the aisle. After all, we had been there for each other for decades.

Soft music played as she made her way down to Roy. Arthur stood beside him with a huge grin on his face. We all knew just how badly Nina and Roy wanted this. It was their profession of love, their symbol of unity. They were pronouncing their affection for all to see. I smiled to myself as I watched them link hands. The justice of the peace, dressed in his plain black suit, began reading.

They didn't seem to pay much attention to him, though. Whenever it was their turn to speak, they did. But during the other moments, they were drowning in each other's eyes. They both said "I do" as if they were more sure of it than anything else in the entire world. And when he pronounced them husband and wife, they collapsed into each other's arms.

"I love you," Nina whispered against his lips.

"I love you, too," Roy replied before pulling her to him.

As soon as the ceremony was over, the justice of the peace hurried away. He seemed to think we were very strange. I couldn't really blame him. Who else had a wedding at eight in the morning?

It didn't take long before Nina and Roy vanished into her bedroom. They would have a honeymoon, but not until his change was complete. They were both ready for it to be done. I watched as Nina closed the door, glimpsing Roy for the last time in his human form. After it was over, he would no longer be a werewolf. His shape-shifting abilities would leave his body, allowing the vampire venom to spread, turning him into one of us.

Only minutes later, Anya walked up to me. "I'm really sorry to leave you alone, but it'll be easier if Roy and Arthur transition at the same time. The sooner we start, the faster it'll be over."

I smiled softly. "Don't worry about me. I'll sit with James."

She looked skeptical. "Are you sure you'll be all right?"

I nodded. "I'll be fine." I glanced toward the door to her room.

She didn't seem entirely convinced but nodded. "All right. It shouldn't take more than a half hour until he passes out. I'll come to check on you then, okay?"

I smiled. "Sure. Don't rush, though."

Anya took Arthur's hand in her own and began pulling him toward her bedroom. She smiled brightly. "Don't worry, we won't."

Arthur gave me a playful smirk before closing the door behind them.

"Have fun," I replied with a grin on my face.

I returned to my room, closing the door behind me. My heart ached, wishing desperately that James was awake. Knowing that Nina and Roy were dissolving into their love for each other made it hard not to be lonely. I tried to think of what it would be like when James woke up.

He would hold me in his porcelain arms, pulling me against him with every ounce of his new strength. I would rest in his love, letting him take care of me. His hard lips would press against mine, and I wouldn't have to worry about bruising him as I kissed him back. I would finally be able to show just how much I loved him. For the first time, I'd really be able to touch him. I wouldn't have to be careful or hesitant. James would truly be mine.

I walked toward his frozen form, stroking his shining hair. It glimmered in the soft light. I pressed a gentle kiss to his lips. We had forever to give each other kisses. Never again would I have to worry about losing him. This love, our love, was infinite.

His lips parted slightly, and my eyes grew wide. I stood perfectly still for several moments, wondering if he'd open his eyes. But no, James fell back into stillness. Even so, it was a sign. It wouldn't be much longer before he woke.

I suddenly remembered that there was something I'd intended to do. Before he woke, I needed to accomplish my task. I'd pondered it for days, wondering if it was the right thing to do. Still, there wasn't any harm in it. It was for myself to release so much of what had been coursing through my busy mind. Hurriedly, I walked to the other side of the room and sat down at my desk.

Chapter 19

In Love With You

It had been months since I'd held a fountain pen. But even after all that time, it still felt natural in my hand. I took out my pale pink stationery, laying several pieces out on the desk before me. With each stroke of my pen, I felt as if I was exposing myself far more than I should. Yet as I thought through each of my words, they seemed to flow directly from my heart. I was pouring my soul out into these letters. There was no reason to hold back; I had no intention of sending them. These pages were filled with everything I would never be able to say. All of the words I had locked in my heart were flowing through my hand, down into my pen, through the ink, and onto the paper. This was for me, to release what I knew I was holding inside. If I kept it hidden away for much longer, I'd explode. I already felt bloated with my thoughts. These feelings that flowed through my veins were overwhelming. I had to release them. Perhaps if I planted them in these letters, they'd stop plaguing me.

But even though the words brought me relaxation, I wondered if I was being too honest. What if I wrote something I didn't want to acknowledge? Maybe some things were best left unsaid. Yet, even so, there was no way that strategy was healthy. But if I didn't plan on acting on some of my feelings, was there any reason to acknowledge them? It might be easier if I pushed them away. The problem was, I'd been trying to do that for days. No matter how hard I attempted to drown them, they kept resurfacing. I simply couldn't get rid of these all-too-honest thoughts.

And so I sat, my letters before me, spilling all of my feelings onto their empty pages. They seemed to breathe as if they were alive. Each time I handed them a new phrase, it was as if they consumed it. My feelings were swallowed within their grasp. It was engrossing. A small bit of weight seemed to lift from my shoulders as I let my words fall from my hands.

When I was finished, I sat completely still. I smelled the overwhelming sweetness from the roses, soft vanilla scent wafting from the candles, and cool air floating through the room. The letters lay before me. It was as if I'd created living creatures. They seemed to stare up at me as I sat contemplating them. I picked the first one up, reading it again.

To my love,

James, I'll never be able to tell you how you made me feel when I saw the complete acceptance within your eyes. You didn't say I was a monster or even a danger. There was total and true trust within your soul. All I received from you in that moment was love. And as I look at you today, I find myself wondering how I became so incredibly fortunate to call you my own.

At first, I was scared. Not for me, but for you. I wanted you to be human, to experience everything life could offer. I thought that making you like me would be the worst possible thing I could do. That's why it took me so long to let myself love you. When I first experienced your heart, your kindness, your gentle soul, I wanted to run into your arms, but I didn't allow myself to. Now I know that I was holding back for nothing. This was meant to be. For some reason, I'll never understand, you were intended to become a vampire. I should have seen that earlier.

Slowly, almost like ice, my heart melted. I realized that I couldn't say no to you. Some things aren't a choice. We can't always choose what happens or how we feel. I never decided to fall in love with you. It just happened. When you showed me how much you wanted my heart, I couldn't reject such a pure desire. I craved your love. There was no doubt in my mind about that. And so, I learned to accept the fact that we didn't stumble into each other by accident. Our souls are linked like chains. They simply can't be moved.

We're incapable of ripping ourselves apart. Even if I spent years trying to do it, I'd never be able to forget you. Your emerald eyes are my safe haven. Truly, you are my love. I want to be able to adore you for the rest of my existence because this is the forever I desire. You're everything I dreamed of.

That night when I agreed to change you, I should have done it. I'd truly intended to, but then things just exploded. My intention had been to protect you, but I didn't. Now I know that I shouldn't have let you out of my sight. I am so, so sorry I failed. Knowing you were in pain was the worst knowledge I'd ever had. I wanted to collapse in on myself, realizing that I'd failed at the one task I'd truly hoped to accomplish.

When we found you, I was furious. I wanted to avenge you, and I did. But seeing you like that, dying in my arms, it made me fall apart. My only focus was saving you. So in that dark, depressing house, I gave you my venom. Then I watched as you began to turn. Your pain from her sick torture vanished as it was replaced by the rush of my bite and then by the terrible sensations of your transformations.

And now, I'm waiting for you to wake up. When you open your eyes, I'll be right there. I'll teach you how to live this life. One day, we'll be able to exist comfortably in our immortality. I'm sure of that. Before you, I'd thought I'd never be happy. Immortality hadn't appealed to me. But now that I have something to live for, I never want this existence to end.

My most fervent wish is to spend forever in your arms. We never have to stop loving each other, and that's glorious. There'll never be a day when we run out of time. From now on, we truly are eternal. And this world we live in, it's beautiful.

So as of today, I'm not holding back. I won't try to

restrain my feelings anymore. My love is all yours. You can have every piece of it. This is it. This is where I give in. When you open your eyes, I'm yours. And so love, I'll wait for you. In only hours, we'll be relishing in each other's love. Until then, I'll think of our forever.

> *With all my heart,*
> *Anne*

I set the first letter down, smiling as I thought of our love. James was the source of bliss, the reason I never wanted to stop living. When he woke, I'd never have to be alone again. We could go anywhere and explore anything we wanted to. And with him by my side, I'd see the world through new colors. Love made everything so much brighter.

I picked up the second letter, slowly bringing my eyes down to it. This one didn't make me smile. Sadness seemed to emulate from the pages.

> *Albert,*

I'm sorry. I'm sorry for how I pictured you, for how I ignored you, for how I misinterpreted who you are. For so long, I only saw the man you pretended to be. I believed the lie. You put on a mask and walk around pretending as if it's your true face. So yes, you fooled me.

You pretend as if you're shallow, flippant, and

completely disinterested. Everyone believes it because you never let anyone get close enough to see who you truly are. But for some reason, you decided to reveal yourself to me. I don't know why you fell for me, but you did. And because of that, I'm the only person who knows your heart. I see through your shell. No matter what you tell the world, you're not half the villain you pretend to be.

I know you give in to your base desires because you're empty. That's something I understand. It's so hard to be alone. And I don't mean physically alone — we both know that's not the case. I mean emotionally. Your body has company, but your soul is starving. It's painful to see. Because when you take that mask off, you look like a wounded, broken man. And oh, how I want to help you.

I need you to know that I didn't walk away from you because I don't enjoy the concept of us. I've contemplated that far too much to ignore my feelings on the matter. The reason I have to say no to you is because I've already given my heart away. James holds everything. I couldn't rip my love away from him if I tried.

There's no choice between the two of you. We just have to accept reality. And for some reason, fate has decided that I belong with him. I couldn't have said no even if I wanted to. There's literally nothing I could possibly do to make myself stop loving him. James, he's the love of my life. I'm so sorry that my loving him hurts you. I never would have chosen that. Pain like what you're experiencing isn't something I would wish on anyone.

But now I'm asking you, telling you that you need to stop pretending. Let the mask go. You have such a beautiful soul. I can't bear to see it hidden. You deserve so much better than living a lie. Be kinder to yourself, Albert. You're more valuable than you know.

As much as I don't want to think about it, there's a part of me that wonders what it would have been like with you. That night in your apartment, I realized that maybe you were right about a lot more than I was willing to admit. I think of my past and of the story you told. We are alike in some ways. There's comfort in that.

But when my thoughts start to drift too far, I remember that none of this was voluntary. James owns my heart. There's no logic or common sense involved. If there had been, none of this would have ever happened. But it all comes down to feelings, to fate. I was meant for James — we belong to each other. You know that I love him.

One day, I hope you find peace. That's what I want for you. I wish you happiness. I'm moving beyond my past, and I know you can move beyond yours too. No matter how we were given this immortal life, whether it be a blessing or a curse, we have to make the most of it. We literally have forever to find happiness. And eventually, I know you'll be successful in your quest.

I wish you every joy,
Anne

A small knock sounded on the door. Moments later, Anya opened it. She wore a light blue silk dressing gown that fell down to her knees. Her spiral curls, which looked entirely gorgeous, tumbled down her back.

"Anne?" Anya whispered.

I turned around, smiling at her. "Yes?"

She walked toward me. "I have something for you."

"What is it?" I replied.

She handed me a sealed envelope with my name neatly written on it. It had an easily identifiable return address. It was from Albert.

"It just arrived," she said.

I nodded, trying to keep myself from ripping it open. Anya looked anxious as if she could sense the tension in my body. My hands were shaking slightly, but I managed to still them. After all, it was just a letter.

"I'll leave you with it," she whispered.

I sunk back into my chair before remembering all that was happening around me. "Anya, how's Arthur?" I asked.

She smiled. "He passed out about five minutes ago. I left him in my bed. The venom's already started to spread, though. I can tell he's cooling down."

I nodded. "Roy?"

She shrugged, smirking slightly. "Nina still hasn't come out of her room."

I grinned. "Well, I guess we'll find out later."

She laughed. "Mhm." Her face turned soft before she added. "How's James?"

I glanced over at him, once again admiring his newly changed form. "I think he'll wake soon."

She nodded, a soft smile still tugging at her lips. "When he does, let me know. I'll try to help as much as I can."

I returned her smile. "Thank you."

She nodded before stepping out of the room, closing the door behind her. Silence surrounded me as I sat alone with my unopened letter and my thoughts. Slowly, I broke the seal.

A piece of gray stationery slid from the envelope. His handwriting was lovely. It looked almost poetic.

My dearest Anne,

I hope you'll forgive me for ending the night the way I did. By now, you'll be headed out of the city and on your way down to Texas. I could have called you or sent you a text, but those both felt wrong. So I retreated back to what I know best. Writing you a letter seemed the most romantic way to tell you my thoughts. Besides, we're both from a time when love wasn't delivered through cellphone towers but rather by spilled, smudged ink.

I know you'll be with him. Perhaps he's already changed. Either way, it doesn't affect what I have to say to you. You know most of it, but I wanted to tell you again. Because no matter how hard I try, I can't get you off my mind.

I've done many things in the past several hours to take my mind away from you. Looking back, they were all useless. No matter how hard I tried, I couldn't stop thinking about your visit. Even as I write this letter, I'm distracted by my thoughts of you.

When you came tonight, I was filled with hope. I thought that maybe I'd been blessed with some sort of miracle. That you changed your mind or realized that I'm better for you. Because Anne, no matter how hard you try to deny it, we fit together.

I've told you how I love you, how I want you to be mine. I've truly never met a woman as fascinating as you. And I know that probably sounds like a lie, but it isn't. I have met incredible people, women included, all over the world. But from the moment I met you, you struck me in a way no one else ever has. So, Anne, I will wait for you.

No matter how long it takes, I'll be here. I won't rush you or tell you that you're making a mistake. There's no point. But what I will do is be patient. Eventually, you'll be in my arms. I'll wait for that day, treasuring the memory of your lips on mine. And when I hold you again, I'll remember just how much the waiting was worth.

So don't be afraid, because no matter what happens, I'm here for you. I'll be there to help, comfort, and love you. And if you find yourself thinking of me, send me a letter back. Just say the words, and I'll be there to bring you home.

I love you, my little dove,

Albert

My chest was tight with anxiety.

Why? Why couldn't he just let me go? It would have been easier for both of us. We didn't need this in our lives. It just brought things to mind that were best not to think about.

And how did he know? How had he become aware of these hidden feelings buried deep within my chest? It was as if Albert was able to stare into my soul. The sensation was more than uncomfortable. I wanted it to disappear, to fade into oblivion.

Maybe if I was lucky, he'd forget about me. I didn't want to see him suffer. Yet he seemed entirely incapable of squelching his feelings. That was something I understood. I wasn't exactly the best at taking a rational approach when it came to emotions. After all, I'd fallen for James.

I picked up all three letters, placing them inside a small box. Carefully, I sealed the container. I had no intention of looking at these for a very long time. The whole purpose had been to release my feelings. If I revisited them too soon, everything would reappear.

I lifted a small piece of the floorboard beneath my desk. It was a secret place, one where I kept things I'd rather not look at. Inside rested a picture of Glen in his military uniform, an image of my parents and I, and a small locket I'd received on my sixteenth birthday. My letters would rest beside these items, hidden within a compartment of my past.

As I once again concealed my precious keepsakes, I attempted to fill my mind with thoughts of James. It wouldn't be long now. Soon, I'd be able to bury my face in his chest. But for now, I'd wait.

Chapter 20
FOREVER

James had begun to stir even more. His body was no longer deathly still but rather looked like he was sleeping. I watched as his fingers twitched, his legs shifted, and he tilted his head to the side. My fingers were laced through his.

Nina and Anya had prepared Roy and Arthur for when they woke. They were still both in the heart of their transformation. Their frigid bodies shook as they lost all semblance of mortality. It was hard for all of us. Even though our memories were vague, we remembered what it felt like to be reborn as immortals. You felt as if you were freezing and burning at the same time. Agony coursed through you as your lungs grew hard and a feeling of suffocation overcame your mind.

I sat beside James, my hand covering his. He was gorgeous. Extraordinary. Entrancing.

"I love you," I whispered.

He seemed to stir a little at the sound of my voice.

If I'd had a beating heart, it might have burst through my chest.

"James, are you there?" I whispered in a questioning tone.

His eyelids began to flicker. Could he hear me? If he could, he needed to know just how much I loved him. James had my heart.

"James, I love you so much. Come back to me," I urged.

My fingers stroked his luscious hair. Maybe he'd finally wake? My breath was ragged as it emerged from my mouth.

"Love?" I asked.

A soft sigh emerged from his lips. I wanted to fall into his arms, but I had to wait until he opened his eyes.

"I'm here, baby, I'm here," I whispered.

Then, I felt as if I might faint. That wasn't possible, though. His lips began to move, his eyelids fluttered, and his muscles twitched.

Moments later, James opened his eyes. I gazed into his emerald galaxies, admiring their expansiveness. I wondered if perhaps I would get lost in them. That might be nice. To just lose myself in his love would be so freeing.

It was odd how giving yourself to someone felt like the most liberating thing you could possibly do. You gave them all of your love, and in turn, it seemed to multiply. Giving felt more like taking. It was so, so glorious. To love and be loved. Was there anything more marvelous?

In that moment, there was no doubt in my mind. James was meant to be my forever. We would spend eternity in this uncontrollable love. Never losing him would be my lifeline, the joy of my heart.

It had felt like ages since he had woken, but it had only been seconds. He hadn't said a word. That was all right—it would take a few minutes for him to process everything. His senses were so new, so full of color and life. He could see everything incredibly clearly, hear each small sound, and feel all that was around him. It was so new, so fresh.

But I couldn't bear to hold myself back any longer; I had been waiting for this for days. All of my loneliness vanished as I looked into his eyes. I would never have to feel abandoned again, never hopeless or undone.

I threw myself into his arms, smelling his fresh, clean scent. His rock-hard chest was firm beneath me as his strong arms came to gently touch my waist. I felt his body around me, his soul flowing against me, and his eyes upon me. Finally, we matched. He and I were the same.

"Oh, James," I mumbled. "I've missed you."

Wrapping my arms around his neck, I fell into a blissful state of peace. Relaxation flooded through me as I felt a true sense of calm overcome my mind.

Happiness had found me. That was what this

was. My world seemed to finally make sense. All of this nightmare, this disaster, had led me to this magical moment. James was mine, forever. I couldn't have asked for anything more.

Coming Soon
Book 2 of the
Shades of Us Trilogy

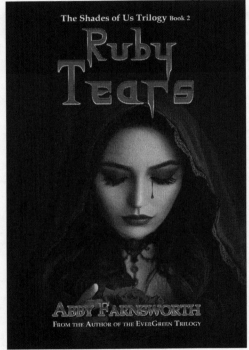

The Shades of Us Trilogy Book 2

Ruby
Tears

ABBY FARNSWORTH
FROM THE AUTHOR OF THE EVERGREEN TRILOGY

Abby Farnsworth is the YA paranormal and urban fantasy romance author of the EverGreen Trilogy. Her books are targeted toward teens and young adults but can be enjoyed by readers of all ages.

She enjoys traveling, history, and reading a good book. When not working on her next novel, she can be found taking long walks exploring the natural world, trying a new recipe, or singing in various ensembles.

She currently resides in West Virginia with her family but adores trips to the beach, mountains, cities, and historical landmarks.

To learn more about Abby, her books, and current projects, take a look at the following:
#authorabbyfarnsworth
#theevergreentrilogy
Instagram: @abbyfarnsworth.writer
Facebook: @abbyfarnsworth.writer.poet

Made in the USA
Columbia, SC
19 August 2023

21683327R00121